To
Jim
Hope you
enjoy the
'57
Ted Williams
Best Wishes
Bill English
H.O.F

50¢

THE
FIND

A NOVEL

BILL ENGLISH

D1207711

Shortstop Press
KENWOOD

Published by **SHORTSTOP PRESS**
P.O. Box 1010, Kenwood, CA 95452

Copyright © 1993 by Bill English
All rights reserved.
No part of this book may be reproduced in any form without
permission from the publisher.

Printed in the United States of America.

Cover and book designed by Joel Wastell
Graphico, Sonoma, CA.

Library of Congress number 92-062485

ISBN 0-9635093-0-6

For Mom and Harrison.

"Suppose there hadn't been any baseball..."
—Lou Gehrig

Chapter One

Butch Wadski had been wild all afternoon so I wasn't exactly looking forward to hitting against him. Butch isn't one of my really good friends and as I stepped into the batter's box he glared at me like I was some kind of insect. Even though the score was eight to six against us, and sort of tight, Butch had a no-hitter going into the seventh. I know what you're thinking—how could we have six runs and no hits, right? Well, it's not that complicated. Wadski had given up over a dozen walks, beaned five batters, and his defense had committed twenty-five errors. Not that his team was all bad. Most of their runs had been earned with ripping blasts that mowed the grass as they went for extra bases.

To tell you the truth, the Kenwood Vines, which happens to be my team, isn't fit to share the same diamond with the Kenwood Hawks. But on this early summer afternoon we were hanging in there much to the amazement of everybody including yours truly.

My name is Mikey Morris and I'm the right fielder for the worst team in the Valley of the Moon. Well, actually I'm not really the first string right fielder. I'm more like a utility man. Which means the coach doesn't put me in unless he absolutely has to. The problem is—I can't hit. Mostly because I'm afraid of the ball. And on this particular afternoon Butch had almost murdered half our infield with his fastball. As I got ready for my turn I could still see Harrison and Jackson sitting on our bench looking dazed.

1

"All right, Morris, show 'em what you've got!"

Our team was down to its last out and I was it. There was no way I needed that kind of pressure in my life

Wadski took a quick look around the bases and noted with a frown that they were still loaded. Old Clive Nuggets was standing on first looking at the dent in his helmet where Wadski had just beaned him with a rising fastball to the temple. The sound had been awful. Like when you foul one off with a metal bat. Clive had gone down like a cold Coke on a hot day.

Wadski turned his attention back to me. I was waving my bat at him but I was standing way back in the batter's box Eddy Wilson, the Hawks catcher, grinned at me from behind his mask as he went into his crouch.

"What's the matter, Morris? You look a little tense."

I tried to ignore him and kept my eyes riveted on Wadski. This time I was determined to hang in there even if it killed me. I'd been swinging at air all my life and I was sick of it. Wadski got set and took one last look over his shoulder at first. As he reared back he gave me a stupid grin with his fat, ugly Mick Jagger lips. They were so chapped, blood was running down his chin. I kept my eyes glued on him as he lifted his leg. The ball came out of a maze of limbs like a white leather bullet and it blew by me and into the catcher's mitt with a confident smack.

"Strike one!"

I stepped out of the box and looked over at my mother. She seemed nervous but hopeful. I was all she had left in the world since the death of my father, and to lose me to a Wadski fastball would be a major family tragedy.

I stepped back in.

Wadski was rubbing the ball for inspiration and as he got set again I could feel my stomach sink. I just couldn't face another strike-out. It was now or never. I crowded closer to the plate and Butch made a note of it. I could almost hear his fat lips crack as he scowled at me. I edged even closer. Wadski went into his windup and threw his heater right at my head. I barely had time to dive out of the way.

"Morris—let it hit you!" my coached screamed.

My mouth was full of dirt but it was my ears I couldn't believe. Did the coach actually expect me to take it on the head for the team? Geez, it was only a game.

"Got something in your mouth, Mikey?" the catcher asked me with a grin.

I tried to smile but my mouth was too dry and full of crud to lube my lips. Wadski had me psyched and everybody knew it. I just wanted to go home and never play baseball again. But of course, that was completely out of the question. I'd rather die than wear the chicken label.

"Come on, Morris, crowd the plate," my coach shouted from the safety of our dugout.

I got back up determined to die for my team. This time I was going to make something happen. Wadski came in with another fastball, and to my utter amazement I could actually see it leaving his hand. I swung with everything I had and was rewarded with a vicious foul tip that caught Eddy Wilson right on his catcher's mask. It was the first time in my whole life that I'd even gotten a piece of a Wadski pitch and everyone seemed stunned. The catcher was on his back moaning in pain. The force of my foul had ripped the mask right off his face. I casually stepped out of the box and gave my cleats a whack with my bat. When I looked over at my mother she seemed thrilled that for once it wasn't her boy eating dirt.

Wadski swaggered to the plate looking real upset. He was shorter than me but still managed to appear massive. His shoulders were so broad he almost couldn't help knocking into me as he extended a hand to his catcher.

"Get up, Wilson, you're not hurt!"

Eddy didn't seem so sure as he ran his fingers over his face like a blind man reading features. When he seemed satisfied that his nose was still in place he put his mask back on and got behind the plate. The crowd cheered his courage and my moment of glory was history. Wadski stomped back to the mound slamming the ball into his mitt in rage. Even a foul tip was an insult off the bat of a geek like me. Butch didn't mind walking a guy or beaning him, and errors never upset him much—but to have a wimp like me actually make contact was more than he could deal with.

I got set again.

Wadski's eyes were blazing as he reared back. A bullet cut the plate in half and my bat never left my shoulder.

"Strike three!"

Boy, do I hate those two words.

"Nice game, Morris," Eddy Wilson sneered as he stepped out into the diamond to hug Wadski.

I tossed my bat against the backstop in disgust. None of the other guys on my team would even look at me as I walked back to our bench. I was a complete loser.

Chapter Two

Later that same night I was lying on my bed staring at the ceiling when it dawned on me that I was never going to play in the Major Leagues. I was only twelve years old and already it looked like I was washed up in baseball. My career seemed over before it had even got started. I turned on my side and looked at the framed photos of my heroes on the wall. These guys were Gods. None of them flinched at the inside fastball.

"Mikey, are you all right?" my mother asked from the other side of my bedroom door.

"Yeah, Mom, I'm fine."

"You want to talk?"

"Not right now."

"Are you sure?"

"Yeah, I just want to be alone."

"Okay, I'll see you in the morning."

I rolled over the other way and stared at my clock radio. The Giants were playing a night game—but I didn't really feel like listening to it. Baseball had turned ugly on me and it was times like these that I really wished I had a father. Even butt-face Wadski had a Dad to slap him on the back.

But I was alone.

My Dad died when I was only two. I've got this old, yellow

newspaper clipping that tells the whole story. I used to read it all the time but lately I haven't had the heart. The article says my father had his head sticking out of a car window when the driver came too close to a telephone pole. Sometimes I still dream about that accident. I see my Dad with his face into the wind like a happy dog. They say he was drunk and probably never knew what hit him. Only in my dream he sees the pole at the last second—but it's too late. I always wake up before his head gets smashed.

Everybody in town knows what happened to my Dad. But not even a jerk like Wadski ever teased me about it. Some things are just off limits. And having a drunk father bash his brains out on a telephone pole is one of them. Once in a while I start to feel sorry for myself and wonder why I got such a raw deal. A kid should have a chance to know his father. But then I think about my mother and I feel better. My mom is the greatest person on the planet. Everybody in Kenwood thinks she's one of the best. She teaches school during the week and then on weekends she cleans other people's houses. At least she used to. But even when she had two jobs we still never seemed to have enough money. I tried to help out. For three years I had a paper route. I got up at four every morning and tossed a hundred of the Santa Rosa daily. I didn't really mind the work. It was sort of nice getting up that early and being the only one on the street. Only sometimes I'd fall asleep at school in the afternoon which made my mother real upset. But both of us knew I couldn't quit my route. I made a hundred bucks a month and we needed every penny of it to make ends meet.

Money was always a major problem.

Not that we were dirt poor or anything. I always got enough to eat. But I knew a lot of rich kids from school and I could see the difference in our lifestyles. Kenwood is the kind of place where people with money live on the hill and look down on the rest of us. But everybody seems to get along okay. People in Northern California try to be cool about stuff like that. And sometimes things happen and the poor do better—but mostly the rich just keep getting richer.

Anyway, like I was saying, I know some rich kids. The reason I know they're rich is because they've got swimming pools, and what I like to call well-stocked refrigerators. For instance, my friend Chad has this immense side-by-side crammed with cold cuts and potato salad. I mean, they've got all this yogurt and fresh fruit. And not just apples and bananas—but seedless red grapes and honeydew melons like you wouldn't believe. And everything is perfectly ripe. I think they buy their stuff at a special market where they have this guy who does nothing but make sure your fruit is just right.

It made me feel sort of lame when I'd have Chad over to my house because all I ever had to give him was peanut butter and jelly sandwiches on cheap white bread. Of course, Chad was way too cool to ever say anything about it. But I knew what he was thinking way down deep. And naturally it was easy for him to be casual about the whole thing since he didn't have to eat peanut butter and jelly every day of his life. Sometimes I even had to eat it for breakfast.

By the end of the month we just didn't have enough money for cereal.

Thank God for Grandma Marie's house on Sunday mornings. Grandma isn't exactly rolling in dough herself—but Mom says she's comfortable. I guess that means she can afford to serve me Danish ham and paper thin pancakes with real maple syrup. Every weekend after church we'd do the same thing. Mom and I would drive over to grandma's house around seven o'clock after I'd finished breaking my back lugging the Sunday edition. As soon as I walked in the door, Grandma Marie would make me stick out my hands so she could check them for ink stains.

"I don't want my grandson rubbing the bad news of the world on my nice clean linen."

It makes sense if you think about it.

Grandma Marie is my father's mother—but since she and Mom are both widows, they're closer than you might imagine. Grandpa Ed died of cancer about nine years ago. I don't remember much about him but they tell me he was some kind of wine merchant. All I know is that Grandma Marie has a lot more money than we do. She owns this big old house surrounded by about a hundred acres of grapes. Someone told me once that the place was worth at least a million bucks—but it really doesn't matter. Grandpa Marie still thinks she's poor. She spends nearly all her time canning jams and jellies. I may have eaten a lot of peanut butter and jelly in my time—but at least the jelly part of it was really something special.

Grandma Marie wins awards for her canning.

She's even got this quilt in her guest bedroom that is made from the different ribbons she's won at the County Fair. I love that quilt. It's all made up of red, blue and yellow satin, and when you sleep under it you feel like a total winner.

Speaking of sleep--I remember that on the night in question I went to bed early because the next day was Sunday and the papers were going to be real heavy.

Chapter Three

I always got up in the dark—but I never complained. To tell you the truth, I sort of liked the stillness of the morning. I could have done my route in my sleep so it gave me plenty of time to think about things. Mostly I thought about what I was going to do with my life. In those three years on the route I guess I imagined myself to be pretty much everything there is to be. You might say I was dreamer. But after a while I stopped thinking about being a pilot or a fireman or anything like that. Not that I had anything against these guys—but I wanted to be something really different. Something special. I wanted to be a guy who did something that nobody else did.

When you're a kid like me who doesn't have a father you don't have to follow in anyone's footsteps.

You also don't have a man to talk to about stuff.

The way I saw it my main problem was that I didn't have much talent for anything in school. I took this vocational test in class one year and it said I should be a journalist. At first I wasn't very hot about the idea, but then Mr. Crane said that maybe I could become a sports writer.

That got me thinking.

Sports writers must have a pretty cool life. And maybe writing about my heroes would be the only way I'd ever see the inside of a Major League club house. At least I'd be hanging around the players.

But I had no idea how you actually became a writer.

I guess you just wrote something.

When you stop and think about it—it's actually a pretty strange thing to do.

Anyway, on this particular Sunday, the day that changed my life forever, the newspapers were loaded with inserts and looked like they weighed about a ton a piece. The guy who drove the truck, his name was Frank, was a pretty cool dude. On Sundays he took the time to drop my papers off in three different locations so I didn't have to haul them all at once. I guess I could have gotten a cart—but I liked the idea of building up my muscles, and besides, a cart cost money.

But even a third of my papers could be a real load on Sundays. I remember on this morning it was all I could do to lift my canvas paper bag over my head. Once the papers settled on my shoulders I felt like I was carrying a load of wet cement. I've got these sloping shoulders anyway, and sometimes I think they might have been caused by all that downward pressure on my bone structure. I can't help worrying that all that weight on me day in and day out might have retarded my development.

So the papers on this Sunday were real heavy and I was practically staggering down the street from the sheer weight of them. I was still feeling wimpy about striking out in my last game and suddenly I found myself crying like a baby. All at once the burden of the papers seemed like more than I could handle. Everything was crushing me like a bug under foot. I got so mad at myself for acting like a geek, I threw the Brown's paper on top of their carport. I had to get a rake and drag it down. While I was doing that, the dog woke up and started barking.

It was just one of those days.

Now the good news about delivering papers is your load gets lighter the farther along the route you are. On Sundays everytime I tossed one I could feel the relief in my muscles. Of course, on the Sabbath I did have to start with three fresh loads—but as each one got lighter I started to soar. Usually by the time I got down to one or two papers, I felt like I could fly or stuff a basketball.

But on this Sunday even after I'd tossed a ton of papers I felt like I was walking on the surface of Jupiter or something.

You probably already know that Jupiter has all this gravity. My Science teacher, Mr. Locke, once told us that the strongest guy in the world couldn't dribble a basketball on Jupiter. Then he turns right around and tells us that anybody in the class could hit a baseball out of Yankee Stadium if it was on the moon. I remember thinking that maybe when the moon had a team I'd be good enough to play on it.

Just kidding, folks.

Back then I was sure I was never going to play professional sports on the moon or anywhere else. Because let me tell you something—I'm not stupid. I knew that Butch Wadski's fastball would be just that much faster on the moon and I'd end up striking out just like I always did.

It's all relative, right?

And I don't fool myself.

A guy without a father has to face reality. You've got to think things out for yourself. And as you can probably tell all ready—I'm thinking most of the time.

It was around that period that I started thinking about girls quite a bit. To be honest with you, I was thinking about them night and day. Well, actually I mostly thought about just one girl. Her name was Kelly. I really liked her but there were a few major problems to the whole thing. First of all, she happened to be the best looking girl in the whole seventh grade, and then to top it all off, she was my best friend's sister.

It made things weird.

And if that wasn't enough—Butch Wadski had the hots for Kelly and acted like he owned her. Of course, since he was about the ugliest guy in Kenwood with the personality of an otter I didn't' think he had much of a chance—but to hear him talk you'd think he and Kelly were practically engaged. Somehow I don't think Butch really knew that much about true love. At least the kind of love I felt for Kelly. I just enjoyed talking to her. When she smiled at me I felt great for a whole week. Now Butch was another story completely. Whenever he talked about Kelly he always mentioned what he called her: *tremendous potential in the chest area.*

Sort of crude—but I've got to admit he had a point. Kelly did have pretty large breasts for an eleven year old, and I can't really fault Butch for making a note of it. I'd be a liar if I told you I'd never noticed them myself. In fact, I even started dreaming about them. And sometimes when I was delivering the papers in the morning, I'd stop thinking about sports and stuff and start thinking about Kelly's breasts. It did funny things to me and made me glad I was the the only one up that early in the morning. Hey, when I say up—I mean awake.

Oh, forget it.

To tell you the truth, as far as I was concerned at the beginning of the summer, Kelly Steele was in the same league as professional baseball. Not even on the moon would she ever fall in love with a strike-out artist like me. After all, her dad is a dentist and one of the coaches on our team. He's a great guy—but sometimes I think he looks at me funny whenever I smile. My teeth are sort of crooked. Not that I'm deformed or anything. But if we'd had money back then I guess I would have gotten braces much earlier. I remember Dr. Steele telling my poor mother we could go either way, and that it was just a matter of *aesthetics.*

At the time my mother said we couldn't afford *aesthetics* and I didn't get the braces. Not that I wanted them or anything. We did have have health insurance—but it never covers everything.

But deep down inside I knew it wasn't my teeth that Dr. Steele was really concerned about. Sometimes when I was dragging my bat back to the dugout after another one of my endless strike-outs I could see his face get this twisted up expression like he had to go to the bathroom real bad. I knew it really bothered him that I couldn't hit because Dr. Steele is one of those guys who only likes winners. His son Chad is what they call a *natural athlete.* He learned how to be one of these *natural athletes* by going to an expensive baseball camp for the last five summers. Chad Steele has actually gotten batting tips from Dusty Baker. Now I ask you—how can the average guy compete against something like that? Having old Dusty check out your swing must really do wonders for your confidence.

Of course most of that *natural athlete* stuff goes right out the window when you're hitting against Butch Wadski. But I must tell you, Chad Steele is the only guy in Kenwood who ever got a homer off of Butch. Naturally, he did it during a big game in front of just about the whole world, including his sister Kelly.

It was the kind of totally awesome event that could make the rest of us feel real unworthy. I mean, when you get right down to it most kids just don't measure up to Chad Steele. And I'm not just talking about baseball. Chad is twelve years old and he already has his very own Porsche. Of course, he can't drive it or anything, but it's his all the same. It's just sitting in his garage like it was the most natural thing in the world. Most of the car is in boxes and I guess as soon as he puts it all together and gets his license he'll be driving around in it. Chad told me once it was some kind of test his father had come up with. So far Chad hasn't done much more than polish the chrome—but he still has almost four whole years to go before he even gets his permit. Then he'll be riding in style.

I remember I was thinking I'd be walking 'til the day I died.

But to get back to this Sunday I was talking about...

When I got done with my route I went home and climbed into bed to try and get some sleep. Since I'm Catholic my grandmother won't let me eat anything, not even a crummy donut, before communion. I guess that wouldn't be much of a problem for the average guy—but for me it was a real pain. I got up so early that by the time seven o'clock rolled around I was half starved to death. After all, I'd already been awake for three hours and lugged a million pounds of newspapers around. A kid needs calories to do stuff like that. On most mornings, Frank, the guy who drove the truck, had a huge box of pastries for his crew. On Sundays he really went all out with the goodies and had this giant thermos of hot coffee to go with the sweets. Sometimes in the early morning, when the light from the street lamp hit him just right, he sort of looked like a devil with eclairs. They told me Frank was some kind of Moslem and that he didn't really know much about communion and tempting Catholics. His favorite line was:

"Coffee keeps the complaints down!"

Anyway, on this Sunday I'd drank two huge cups of java and was feeling as wired as a hamster by the time I got back to my house. I couldn't sleep so I took a shower and then started looking through my baseball cards. I love baseball cards. They make me feel close to my heroes, and they're also a pretty good investment. I've been buying them for about five years and some of my rookie cards have really gone up in value. Will Clark is my favorite player. *The Thrill* is pretty much the main man around here. The thing I like best about him is that he always seems to come through in the clutch. When the Giants need a run and they have guys on base, Will makes this weird monkey face that doesn't look exactly human. Sometimes when I'm watching him on the tube I study that face real close and it's a little bit scary. Like a monster or something. Will calls it his game face. I'm always hoping it will turn up on his new cards—but so far he's only smiling.

Like I was saying, I've got tons of cards. More than anybody else I know. I've even got more cards than Chad because I've been buying them for so long. I have five Topps Traded Will Clark rookies that went for about ten bucks a piece. At the time it seemed like a lot of money.

Around six o'clock that Sunday morning my mother peeked into my room.

"Mikey, are you awake?"

"Yeah, Mom, I'm just looking at my cards."

Even without makeup my mother was the best looking woman in Kenwood. It had something to do with her eyes and smile. When she grinned everything in her face lit up and you couldn't help but smile back at her.

"You'd better get dressed. We've got to leave for your grandmother's house in twenty minutes."

"Okay."

The thing I hated most about going to church was that I didn't have anything really cool to wear. Not only that—but everything I did have was way too small. All my slacks were these high water jobs that came up over my shoes by about three inches and my sweaters were all pulled out of shape because I'd tried to stretch them to fit. My mother was always telling me that God didn't care what you wore in his house—but then maybe God was never in love with Kelly, or had a friend like Chad.

Like I mentioned before, most of the time the different classes of people mix pretty well in Kenwood—but on Sundays things are a little different. It's almost as if people think they can impress God with their fancy clothes and cars. To give you an example, normally Dr. Steele drives an old Toyota truck around. I've noticed a lot of rich guys do that. I asked my mother why a guy like Dr. Steele would drive an old truck and she told me that the doctor didn't wish to appear pretentious. I asked her what that meant and she told me to look it up in the dictionary. So I did. I guess it means showing off, and that really confused me. Because on Sundays around here everybody is showing off their blessings with a vengeance. The only problem with that was my blessings were all a size too small or had a rod knock. Not that I'm complaining, but once when my mother parked our Pinto right next to Dr. Steele's long black Mercedes, I couldn't help but notice that blessings seem to come in a lot of different models and colors. Some moments stick with you and I'll never forget getting out of my mother's heap of junk and catching my own reflection in the mile deep paint of Dr. Steele's car. I looked like such a geek it made me want to crawl under a bridge and become a troll.

I guess I was just jealous.

Which is a pretty ungrateful and rotten way to feel right before you go to communion—but I couldn't help myself. And the Mercedes was only part of the problem. Here I was looking like a nerd and Chad was wearing a different sweater every time I saw him. He had so many outfits you could never predict what he was going to have on. But me, I always looked the same. Like a weed that needed transplanting to a bigger pot. It really made me feel weird when I walked down the aisle.

Man, was I a major head case, or what?

But to get back to the point, Grandma Marie was standing by her gate like she always was when we pulled up. Grandma was another one who always looked exactly the same. She pulls her white hair back into a bun and never fails to wear black. Grandma is almost eighty but she still has all her marbles. As I helped her into the car that morning she looked at me with a funny expression on her wrinkled old face.

"Your father has been dead ten years today," she said as if he might be coming back. I stared at her in confusion and didn't know what to say. My mother looked over at her.

"Maybe we should visit his grave after church?"

Grandma Marie shook her head.

"Not a chance, daughter. I've got no intention of going to the cemetery on a beautiful day like today. I just brought it up because I've decided Mikey is old enough to have a few of his father's things."

"Things?" my mother repeated.

"That's right. Bud left a trunk in the attic."

"And you're just getting around to telling us about it now?" my mother asked in amazement.

Grandma Marie looked out the window at her grapes. They were looking pretty good.

"It's just a bunch of kid stuff. I haven't even looked at it since Bud died."

I leaned over from the back seat.

"What kind of kid stuff?" I asked.

"Old toys. Maybe a bat and glove."

I smiled and leaned back in my seat.

"Cool," I whispered to myself.

"What's that Mikey?"

"I just said cool."

My mother smiled at me in the rear view mirror.

"I guess it would be nice for you to have something to remember your father by."

"Uh, huh," I mumbled.

Chapter Four

Time moves slow when you're sitting in a pew. Now I believe in God and all that, but usually when I'm in church my mind wanders to other things. On this particular Sunday not even the back of Kelly Steele's head, which on most occasions would have kept me amused for an entire High Mass, could hold my attention. I just couldn't sit still because I was thinking about that trunk waiting for me back at grandma's house.

I guess to most guys something like that would be no big deal. I mean, who really cares about an old used glove and a bat? But to a kid like me, who never really knew his father, it was the greatest thing that could happen. Almost like my father was coming back from the dead or something.

At least a small part of him was.

By the time mass was over my grandmother was more than a little ticked off at me. As we got back into the Pinto she sort of looked down her nose at me, and it was then I noticed she was kind of scary if you looked real close.

"What's wrong, Grandma?"

"To tell you the truth, Mikey, I'm not very happy with the way you were acting in church. You didn't pay one bit of attention to what Father James was saying. I'll bet you have no idea what the sermon was about."

I smiled.

"It had something to do with greed," I said as I looked down at my scuffed dress shoes.

Grandma Marie shook her head and fastened her seat belt.

"I guess you're all worked up over that silly trunk from your father?"

I nodded.

"That's right, Grandma."

"Well, don't go getting your hopes up. It's not like it's a legacy or an inheritance. Your father had no idea he was going to die so young. So don't go expecting any letters filled with fatherly wisdom. All you're getting is a bunch of stuff from when he was a boy. For all I know it could be nothing but moth-eaten junk."

My mother turned and looked at me in the back seat.

"But it *is* your father's junk," she said with a smile.

When we got back to the house grandma insisted we eat breakfast before we went up into the attic. I was beginning to get this strange feeling in my stomach and my pancakes went down like cement. Grandma Marie tortured me by taking her time drying the dishes. After about a million years she finally turned to me with a nod.

"Okay, Mikey, let's open the trunk."

As we lowered the ladder to the attic it creaked like no one had used it in years.

"When was the last time you were up here?" I asked my grandmother.

"I guess it's been a while. Maybe ten years."

"Ten years! How long has the trunk been up there?"

My grandmother began to slowly climb the ladder. She was old but she could still get around pretty good.

"Well, let me think. If your father were alive he'd be forty-six years old. You know he was quite a bit older than your mother when they got married. So I guess the trunk has been up here for almost forty years."

"Forty years!"

"Your grandfather and I got it for Bud when he was just a toddler. Whenever he got tired of something we'd throw it in the trunk."

"Wow—it's going to be like a time capsule!"

"Mikey, remember what I said. Don't go getting your hopes up."

It was too late for that. My hopes were as high as a McGwire pop up. As I stood in the dim light of the attic I could feel my heart pounding in my chest. Grandma Marie pulled a cord and an old bare light bulb flickered to life.

"Goodness, I can't believe that still works," she said.

I looked around in the dusty light.

"Where's the trunk, Grandma?"

"I think it's over there behind that pile of furniture."

I started moving stuff out of the way. Sure enough, the trunk was sitting under a dining room table. I pulled it out into the center of the attic and took a good look at it.

"Wow, this thing is cool."

The trunk was all black patent leather and had these big brass hinges.

"Shall I open it?" I asked.

Grandma Marie sat down in a chair.

"That's why we're up here, kiddo."

I fell to my knees before the trunk. My hands were trembling as I tried to lift the lid.

"I think it's locked," I said with a frown.

"Really?"

"I can't open it."

My grandmother looked thoughtful for a moment.

"Mikey, go down to the big roll top desk in the library and look in the top drawer on the right hand side. I think there's a ring of keys there."

"Got it."

I was in such a hurry I almost fell out of the attic. Now that the big moment had arrived I couldn't stand to wait another second. I had to know what was in that trunk. I found the ring of keys just where my grandmother said they would be and headed back to the attic.

"Are these the ones?" I asked.

"Yes, now let me see..."

Grandma Marie began to finger the keys like they were rosary beads. I could see from her eyes that each one held some kind of memory.

"Try this one," she said at last.

The key was long and simple. I slipped it into the brass

lock and it seemed to fit, but when I tried to turn it nothing happened.

"Here, let me try," my mother said. A look of determination came over her face as she twisted the key. All at once there was a loud click and the lock sprang open.

"Okay, Mikey, it's all yours."

As I lifted the lid a wave of disappointment washed over me. The trunk seemed to be filled with nothing but old rags. I began to toss them aside like a dog digging for a bone. Before long things started to look up.

"Hey—here's an old Duke Snider bat!"

"Is that good, Mikey?"

"Yeah, it's sort of cool."

Next I found a Willie Mays glove and a complete little league uniform.

"Was this my father's?" I asked.

"I believe it was."

I dug deeper. Near the bottom, my heart skipped a beat. Three black binders wrapped in clean rags sat in the corner of the trunk. I forced myself to take a long breath of the stale air before I even touched them.

"Mikey, what is it? You look as pale as a ghost."

"I think I found something good."

"What?" my mother asked.

I took one of the binders from the trunk and slowly opened it.

"OH WOW!"

Chapter Five

You hear a lot about how a guy's eyes bugged out of his head, but until that Sunday, I guess I never really knew what people were talking about. Now I do. It's funny, because just that week we'd been studying the eye in school, so I knew it was my cornea's that were ready to pop out of their sockets. I felt like a cartoon character. My eyes just couldn't get enough of what was in my lap, and I felt like I might faint.

"Mikey—what is it?" my mother asked in alarm.

I was speechless. My mouth began to move but no words came out. I kept staring at the first page of the folder in disbelief. There—right under my nose—were twelve of the most perfect 1952 Topps cards I'd ever seen. Absolute blazers! Now a lot of kids my age have no interest in old baseball cards—but I do. I knew *exactly* what I was looking at. Three cards in the center row were the fabled Mickey Mantle Topps rookie . There was also a Mathews' rookie. A Willie Mays. A Pee Wee Reese. And a Roy Campanella.

I carefully turned the page.

More mint superstars stared out at me. I began to shake as I came to the 1953 cards. More Mantles and Berras. More of everybody. All three binders were stuffed with mint cards. I forced myself to turn away from my find and looked up at my mother and grandmother.

"Mom, you can forget about scrubbing toilets."

"What?"

"We're rich," I said with a grin.

Grandma Marie looked confused.

"Grandson, what are you talking about?"

I stood up and carried the binder with the Mantle Topps rookies over to them as if it were some kind of Holy Bible. My mother and grandmother stared at it in bewilderment.

"You see those three cards in the middle row? The Mickey Mantles?"

"Yes," my mother answered."

"Those three cards are the most valuable Topps ever issued."

Grandma Marie smiled.

"Oh, that's nice, Mikey."

My mother wasn't so casual about the whole thing. I'd recently read her an article in the newspaper about the value of old baseball cards. The *Wall Street Journal* had called them the best investment of the eighties.

"How much are they worth?" my mother asked calmly.

I took a real close look at the cards. One of them was slightly off-center—but the other two were perfect. The corners were razor sharp and the colors were blazing.

"This one is a little off-center. It's probably only worth around $35,000..."

"Thirty-five thousand *dollars?*" my mother gasped.

"Yeah, but these other two are gem mint. I'll bet we could get a lot more for them."

Grandma Marie frowned.

"Mikey, are you trying to tell us those pieces of cardboard are worth as much as a nice car?"

"That's right, Grandma."

"Are you sure about that?"

"Well...I've got a price guide at home. I could show you."

"And what about the rest of the cards?"

"They're worth a lot, but not as much as the Mantle. "

We all stood in silence for a moment.

"How much to you think we're talking about, Mikey?" my mother asked at last.

I grinned.

"Tons, Mom, tons..."

My mother gave me a huge hug.

"Mikey, I love you."

"I love you too, Mom."

Grandma Marie seemed like she was in shock.

"What are you going to do now, Grandson?"

I closed the binder.

"We need to talk to an auctioneer."

"An auctioneer?" my grandmother repeated with respect.

"That's right, Grandma. We're going to auction a few of these puppies!"

Chapter Six

My stomach was real nervous as we drove back over to our house. Nothing like this had ever happened to me before and I was more than a little confused by it all. Why was I getting such a major break? Was this one of those blessings people were always talking about? I held the binders in my lap and couldn't help but smile. Outside the car window the whole world looked better. The morning seemed more friendly and bright. For the first time in my life I felt like I was in control of things.

My mother and grandmother seemed dazed by what was happening and looked straight ahead as we drove across Kenwood. Neighbors waved like always. None of them knew our secret.

Things had changed in an instant.

Mikey Morris was now one rich kid!

I jumped out of the car as soon as it stopped and dashed into the house. By the time my mother and grandmother caught up with me I had already got the *Beckett's* price guide out and was poring over it to see *exactly* how rich I really was. *Beckett's* is the Bible when it comes to sports card prices. The magazine is published once a month and lists card values all the way back to the 1948 Bowman set.

"Whoa!" I gasped.

"Mikey, what is it? Did you make a mistake?" my mother asked.

"Not really."

I held my finger under the price for the 1952 Topps Mantle rookie.

"Thirty-five thousand!" my grandmother whispered.

I nodded.

"Yeah, $35,000 for near mint," I explained.

"I'm not following you, Grandson."

"Two of my cards are mint, not near mint."

"What does that mean?" my mother asked.

"Mint cards can be worth two or three times more than near mint ones."

"Mikey, what are you saying?"

"I'm saying that two of these Mantles could be worth as much as $70,000!"

Grandma Marie cleared her throat.

"Well...how do you tell the difference between mint and near mint?" she asked with interest.

"It has to do with how sharp the corners are and the gloss and centering. Stuff like that."

My mother and grandmother stared down at the Mantle cards as if they were some sort of holy relic. I could see the doubt in their eyes. How could these cards possibly be worth so much money? After all, they were just pieces of cardboard. I slowly ran my finger down the list of names until I came to the last card in the series. It was the Mathews' rookie.

"How come that one is only worth $2,700?" my mother asked in confusion.

"*Only* $2,700?" my grandmother repeated in disbelief. "We're talking about something your father paid a penny for! We're talking about something little kids collect!"

I smiled at my mother.

"The Mantle card is the key card in the set."

"Why?"

"Because Mickey Mantle is a legend. He's the main hero to guys of that generation. And those are the guys with the big money to spend on cards right now."

"What else have you got?" my grandmother asked with mounting excitement.

"There's a blazing mint Mays."

"What's he worth?"

"In this condition? I bet I could get $4,000 for him."

I turned to the 1953 set.

"I've also got two Mantles from '53."

"What do they go for?"

"Around $3,000."

Grandma Marie took off her glasses and cleaned them carefully.

"Are you telling us that the 1952 Mantle is worth ten times more than the 1953 Mantle?"

"That's right."

"Why such a difference?"

"Because the '52 Topps Mantle is classified as a rookie card. Although it isn't really a rookie card—they just call it that because it's the first Mantle put out by Topps. Rookie cards are usually the most valuable."

"Even when they're not really rookie cards?" my grandmother asked in confusion.

I smiled.

"I know it seems a little weird—but it all makes sense in a way."

Grandma Marie didn't look so sure as she sat down on my bed. She stared at the binders for a long time before she finally said:

"Mikey, I don't know a rookie card from a hole in the ground—but one thing is clear to me. We're dealing with an awful lot of money here."

I was already clicking numbers into my pocket calculator. I stopped for a second and looked up at my mother and grandmother.

"I think I'd like to be alone for a while."

"What?" my mother sputtered. "Mikey, are you actually kicking us out of your room?"

"Mom, don't put it like that."

"Well...how would you like me to put it?"

"I just want to add up the numbers."

"Add up the numbers!" Grandma Marie repeated in astonishment. "The kid is already beginning to sound like some kind of accountant."

"Mom, I need to concentrate!"

My mother and grandmother looked at each other. I could see that deep down they were pleased that I was acting like a man.

"Okay, Mikey, we'll leave you alone."

"Thanks. This won't take all day."

As soon as they closed the door I fell back on my bed and held a pillow over my face to muffle my screams of joy. My feet were pumping the air like I was beating out an infield single as I howled with pleasure.

Chapter Seven

The total was impressive.

I checked it three times because I couldn't believe my eyes.

Two hundred and fifty thousand dollars.

And that was just the star cards.

I also had hundreds of valuable commons. I stared at the total and tried to come to grips with such a massive figure. Over a quarter of a million bucks was almost more than I could deal with. I began to pace as my mind raced like a calculator with fresh batteries. At a $100 a month it would take me almost three centuries to earn that much cash on my paper route.

I picked up the phone and dialed my boss. A sleepy voice came over the line.

"Hello."

"Frank, this is Mike Morris."

"How you doing, kid?"

"I'm doing pretty good, Frank."

"What's up?"

"I want to quit my route."

"Gee...I'm sorry to hear that. Are you sure?"

"I've never been so sure of anything in my life."

Frank was quiet for a moment.

"Mikey, this is pretty short notice. Can you stick around for another week and help me break in a new kid?"

"Yeah, sure, Frank, but only one more week. I've got a lot of sleep to catch up on."

"Okay, thanks for calling. I'll see you tomorrow."

I hung up and felt like a large rock had been lifted from my chest. My days of breaking my back before dawn would soon be history. In one week Mikey Morris would start sleeping 'til noon. Maybe I'd even quit school. Now that I was rich I could get myself a tutor, and maybe even a personal trainer. From now on my time was going to be my own.

My daydreams were interrupted by my mother's voice from beyond the door.

"Mikey, how about some lunch?"

"Sounds good, Mom."

Three hours had gone by in a flash. I took a red felt pen and circled the magic number that told the world my net worth. Then I folded the piece of paper and put it in the breast pocket of my shirt. I wanted everyone to be sitting down when I dropped the bombshell. I walked into the kitchen and took my usual place at the head of the table.

"How are those numbers adding up?" my mother asked as she placed a peanut butter and jelly sandwich in front of me. I stared down at the food and frowned.

"Mom, I'm sick and tired of peanut butter and jelly! Don't you have anything else?"

My grandmother looked hurt.

"Mikey, I thought you loved my jelly."

I saw the expression on her face and adjusted my attitude.

"Grandma, you know I love your jelly, but to tell you the truth, I've had enough of it for a while. Why don't we all go to the Kenwood restaurant and pig out?"

My mother gazed down at her apron. The look on her face told me I was skating on thin ice.

"Mikey, I think you'd better eat your sandwich. I'm not going to waste good food."

I carelessly lifted the sandwich to my mouth and took a half-hearted bite.

"Okay, Mom, but tonight we eat in style."

Grandma Marie lofted an eyebrow.

"Are you buying, Grandson?"

I smiled.

"Of course."

"Feeling rich, are we?"

I took the piece of paper out of my pocket and tossed it on the table. It fluttered open like a butterfly coming out of a cocoon. The circled number glowed like a winning lottery ticket.

"Oh, my..." Grandma Marie whispered.

"Is that $250,000?" my mother asked unable to believe her eyes.

"That's just a rough guess, Mom. I think it might come to a lot more."

"More than $250,000?"

"Yeah."

"But, Mikey, that's enough to pay off the mortgage on this house and then some."

I took another bite of my sandwich.

"I don't know much about that, Mom, but I do figure we can afford some Danish ham and potato salad. Maybe even some roast beef."

My mother looked like she was about to cry.

"Mom, what's wrong?"

"Oh, Mikey, I'm sorry you had to eat so many peanut butter and jelly sandwiches. I did my best."

I stood up and put my arm around her.

"Hey, Mom, I'm the one who should be saying he's sorry. I didn't mean to hurt your feelings. I'm acting like a real geek."

Grandma Marie was drumming her fingers on the table.

"Hey, you two, forget about the sorries. We've got more important things to worry about than how many peanut butter and jelly sandwiches Mikey has had to eat in his life. I think we'd better get these cards into a safety deposit box first thing tomorrow morning. They're too valuable to keep around the house."

I frowned.

"Well, I guess that would be okay, Grandma, but first I want to test the waters."

"Test the waters?" my mother repeated.

"I'd like to take a card into Santa Rosa and see if I could sell it."

Grandma Marie looked concerned.

"I thought you said you wanted to auction them, Mikey?"

I nodded.

"I do want to auction most of them—but right now I'd like to get my hands on some fast cash. I just quit my paper route."

My mother looked stunned. I guess she was still operating on the poverty level.

"You quit your route?"

"Mom, I don't need it anymore."

"But that's a $100 a month!"

"Chicken feed," I said as I tossed the rest of my sandwich onto my plate.

My mother and grandmother looked at each other.

"Mikey, you're moving pretty fast," Grandma Marie said.

I grinned.

"Trust me, ladies."

As soon as I finished my lunch I disappeared back into my room to get the binders. I placed them on the kitchen table and slowly began to flip through the pages. The cards still took my breath away.

"I guess this Campanella will do the trick," I said as I carefully removed it from the plastic page. I took one of my McGwire rookie cards from a plexi screw down and replaced it with the Hall of Fame catcher. Once Campy was encased in the holder he looked like a jewel in a fine setting. I held him up so my mother and grandmother could see.

"Impressive, Mikey."

"Yeah...it sure is."

"Now what?"

"Let's hit the road," I said brightly.

"What are you going to do with the rest of the cards while we're gone?" my grandmother asked with real concern.

I thought about that for a minute.

"I guess we'd better bring them with us. We can lock them in the car."

"Do you think that's a good idea?"

"Mom, nobody is going to break into a twenty year old Pinto covered in primer spots. You'd have to pay someone to steal that thing. We'll just put the binders in a paper bag."

My mother looked at me in a strange new way.

"Mikey, I hope this money isn't going to change you too

much."

    I grinned.

    "Mom, relax, I'm still the same old Mikey."

    My mother tried to smile.

    "I just wish you hadn't quit your route so fast."

    I got to my feet.

    "Who needs it. Let's get going."

Chapter Nine

Most of the time I bought my cards at a place called Mr. Baseball near the downtown mall. The owner was some old guy who had actually seen Willie Mays play at Seal's Stadium. He had one of the only shops in Santa Rosa that handled old and expensive cards. As we walked into the store, Billy, the guy who owned it was sitting behind the counter looking glum. The sight of me sandwiched between my mother and grandmother seemed to cheer him up. Maybe it was my birthday and the ladies would be springing for a full set.

"Mikey, how you doing buddy?"

Billy was one of those guys who always remembered everybody's name. Someone told me once that before he got into baseball cards he'd sold insurance.

"I'm doing pretty good, Billy."

"And who are these fine ladies?"

I made the introductions.

"Nice to meet you. Now how can I help today?"

I got right to the point. I took the Campy out of my pocket and slid it across the the top of the glass display case.

"I was thinking about selling this," I said as casually as I could manage.

Billy perked right up.

"Well, well, what have we got here, Mikey?"

"A '52 Campy."

"So I see."

Billy gave it a quick look like he saw such rarities every-day.

"Nice card, Mikey. How much you want for it?"

"I'll let it go for full book."

Billy looked like I'd just punched him in the face.

"Mikey, Mikey, Mikey. I can't give you full book. How would I make any money? I've got my rent. My insurance. My lights."

"Billy," I said softly, "maybe you'd better take the card out of the plexi and have a really good look at it. The thing is gem mint."

"Yeah, okay."

Billy got out a screw driver and removed the card. He began to pore over it with a large magnifying glass.

"Nice surface. Plenty of gloss."

"It's perfect, Billy."

"Where'd you get it?" he asked.

"It belonged to my father. It hasn't been touched in years."

Billy looked up from the card with a funny expression on his oily face. His eyes were bright with greed.

"You got anymore cards like these?"

"Maybe," I said.

"If you do, I'd like to have the first look at them."

I leaned on the counter.

"Then give me a good price, Billy."

"Yeah, sure thing."

"You got a *Beckett's* guide handy?"

"Right here, Mikey, my man."

I flipped open the magazine.

"It says right here, Billy, that pre-1980 cards in mint condition are worth 110-150 percent of near mint value."

Billy peered down at the card.

"Sure, sure, but this card isn't mint."

I twitched a bit.

"What's wrong with it?" I asked with an edge to my voice.

"It's lost some of it's luster."

Billy was playing games and we both knew it. The Campy was so blazing it looked three dimensional. All the corners were razor sharp and it was perfectly centered.

"Admit it's gem mint or I'm walking," I said firmly.

Billy picked up the card. All at once he began to look at it as if he owned it."

"How much is full book anyway?" he asked.

"Two thousand."

"What about if I give you $1,500?"

"Two thousand."

"What about $1,800?"

I shrugged.

"Okay, Billy, I'll give you a hundred bucks. You can have the card for $1,900 cash."

Billy had his wad out so fast it made my head spin. He peeled off nineteen hundred dollar bills and tossed them on the counter. My mother and grandmother stood in slack-jawed amazement as I counted out my money.

"Good deal, Billy."

"Yeah, don't forget what I told you. If you've got anymore of these give me a call."

"We'll see," I said as I stuffed the cash in my shorts.

"That's it," my grandmother exclaimed. "No sales tax. No receipt."

I smiled at my grandmother.

"We're out of here, Grandma."

"Hey, Mikey, don't go running off."

I turned back to Billy at the last moment like Columbo.

"One more thing, Billy. How much do you think I could get for the Mantle from the same series?"

Sweat began to bead on Billy's forehead.

You mean the Topps Mantle rookie?"

"Yeah, that's right?"

"In this kind of condition."

"Gem mint."

"Are you telling me you've got one?"

"Maybe."

Billy didn't say anything at first. He just stared at his new Campy for a long time before he spoke.

"Is it centered like this one?"

"Perfectly centered."

"Well, a few months ago they auctioned one at Wolffers for $62,000. They got more than twice the book for it."

"Did you say $62,000?" my grandmother gasped.

"That's right, lady."

"For one baseball card?"

"You got it."

My grandmother put her arm around me and shoved me out the door.

"Let's get out of here," she giggled.

We were all laughing our heads off by the time we got back to the Pinto.

"Did you hear what that man said?" my grandmother asked in amazement. "Sixty-two thousand dollars for one Mickey Mantle rookie card! And Mikey has three of them!

I climbed into the back seat. The wad of money was hot and sweaty in my pocket.

"Where to now, Mikey?" my mother asked.

I grinned at her through the rear view mirror.

"The mall, Mom, the mall!"

Chapter Ten

You'd be amazed how much better the world looks when you've got a hundred dollar pair of Ray Ban sunglasses perched on your nose. Not to mention the fact that I was walking on air in a brand new pair of high-top Nikes. It took me about three hours to blow the entire Campy windfall at Macy's. I got my mother seven new dresses with matching shoes and some cool new shorts and T-shirts for myself. I even bought a bra for my grandmother.

Things were definitely looking up.

"Mikey, you look like a movie star in those glasses."

I tossed back my blond hair with a jerk of my head.

"It's my Tom Cruise look, Mom."

Grandma Marie checked me out from head to toe.

"You sure spent that money in hurry, Grandson."

I smiled and looked at my reflection in the window of a department store. I remember thinking that maybe I should get my teeth capped.

"There's plenty more where that came from, Grandma."

My mother looked sheepish.

"Mikey, in all the excitement I let you go a little nuts. But from now on you're going to have to let your grandmother and I handle the money."

I lowered my sunglasses and peered over the frames.

"Mom, the cards belong to me."

"I know they do. But you're only twelve years old. There's

no way we're going to turn you loose with over a quarter of a million dollars. We'll have to set up a trust fund."

"A trust fund!"

"That's right."

I slammed my sunglasses back up my nose.

"Mom, I want to start living the good life right now! I've already got plans for that money."

"Plans?" my grandmother repeated.

I looked at both of them and decided my best move was to cool it for a while. No sense revealing everything before it had time to gel in my brain.

"We can talk about all that later," I said. "Right now we've got to get ourselves some new wheels."

"Mikey, what are you saying?" my mother asked.

"We need a new car, Mom."

"But you just spent all your money."

"You ever hear of credit?"

By this time we'd gotten back to the Pinto. It sat in the mall parking lot looking old and faded.

"This thing is a death trap," I said.

Grandma Marie nodded her agreement.

"The boy is right. I worry about you driving around in a Pinto."

"Well, I'm not going into debt to a bank," my mother said firmly.

Grandma Marie climbed into the car.

"I'll lend you the money," she said.

"You will?"

"Of course. Mikey is good for it."

I grinned.

"You got that right, Grandma."

"But I don't even know what to buy," my mother said in confusion.

"We're going to get a Ford Explorer," I beamed.

"A what?"

"A green Eddie Bauer model."

"I thought Eddie Bauer made clothes."

"He also designs trucks."

"You want to get a truck?" my grandmother asked.

"Yeah, they're real cool."

"This is nuts," my mother moaned.

"Mom, I'm not riding around in this piece of junk anymore."

My mother attempted to adjust the rear view mirror and it came off in her hand. She smiled and turned to me.

"I guess it is sort of used up, isn't it?"

"Abused is more like it. The Ford dealership is on the Corby Auto Row off the freeway. Let's get moving."

The Pinto must have sensed that it was going to the glue factory because it started to cough and buck even worse than normal. As we pulled into the lot no one came out to greet us. The Pinto marked us as trailer trash.

"There's an Explorer in the showroom, Mom."

"Mikey, that thing is huge."

"You'll love it," I promised.

We walked inside and my mother immediately suffered massive sticker shock.

"Twenty-two thousand dollars!"

"Mom, that's the cheap model."

"The cheap model!" my mother giggled on the verge of a meltdown.

A salesman walked up to us like we were slime. He knew what we drove up in and he wasn't impressed.

"May I be of help?" he asked.

Grandma Marie stared at him with a cold eye.

"Perhaps you can, young man. My grandson wants to buy a truck."

"Isn't he a little young to drive?"

"I didn't say he wanted to drive it. I just said he wanted to buy it."

The salesman looked a little mixed up—but he wasn't about to turn away a deal during a major recession.

"So, what's your name, son?"

"Mikey."

"Well, Mikey, my name is Walt Wiseman. Now what kind of a truck were you looking for?"

"I want a dark green Eddie Bauer Explorer with every option you can pile on it."

Mr. Wiseman looked impressed.

"Well, you certainly sound like you know what you want. And I think we may have just the ticket in the back."

"Great."

Old Walt wasn't lying. Our new truck was sitting on the lot behind the dealership like it had been waiting for us to arrive.

"This one cost almost $30,000," my mother whispered.

"Yes, but it has leather and a CD player, and power everything you can imagine," Walt crooned with enthusiasm.

My grandmother walked around the truck like it was a casket.

"We'll give you $24,000 cash for it," she said at last.

Mr. Wiseman looked offended.

"Madam, that's a pretty low offer."

Grandma Marie began to walk out.

"Now wait a minute. Why don't we talk about this in my office?"

"There's nothing to talk about, sonny boy. But I'll tell you what we'll do. If you agree to my terms right now I'll have my daughter-in-law throw in that fine Ford classic that we drove up in. You know, Mr. Wiseman, the model that blows up like a bomb when hit from the rear."

Walt tried to smile.

"I'll be happy to submit your offer to my sales manager."

Grandma Marie smiled back baring her false teeth.

"You can submit to anything you want—but you're not getting anymore money out of us. This is strictly a take it or leave it deal."

Walt ushered us into his office. He brought in another man who tried to get more money out of my grandmother—but they didn't have a chance. They caved in like a sand castle when we started to walk out the door. Two hours later the truck had been washed and filled with gas and we were riding in style.

"Boy, this thing is pretty nice," my mother admitted.

"Yeah, but we need some sounds."

"Sounds?"

"We don't have any CDs."

"Mikey, you can listen to the radio."

I folded my arms over my chest.

"Mom, I didn't pay all this money to listen to the radio!"

"Mikey, you're out of control."

"I want Madonna!"

My mother frowned.

"Since when have you started thinking about Madonna?"

I blushed.

"Well, it doesn't have to be Madonna."

Grandma Marie shrugged.

"What the heck. We just spent a fortune on this thing. We may as well go whole hog."

We spent another $500 at the record store. By the time we got back to the house I owed my grandmother almost half of one of my Mantle rookies.

But I got my Madonna.

Chapter Eleven

If kids had any idea what adults talk about after we went to bed--none of us would ever sleep again. I mean, here I was on top of the world. I had nearly a zillion dollars worth of mint baseball cards under my bed and I was feeling great. After all, how could I have known about the nightmare that would be waiting for me at the breakfast table the next morning? Like a clueless fool I was walking on air as I did my route the next day in my new shoes. I would have worn my shades too, but it was still dark outside, and besides I had this new kid with me. His name was Josh and he was a year younger than me. Talk about lame. This guy actually thought it was cool to be up before the sun. I guess it is the first time—but try doing it for three straight years. It's enough to warp your outlook.

But getting up early would soon be history for yours truly.

And besides, most of the real work was over.

Now it was Josh breaking his back under the load. As I walked the route that morning it was all I could do not to brag about how rich I was. When Josh asked me why I was quitting I told him I was planning on concentrating on my sports career.

He seemed pretty impressed.

But my great mood faded like a split finger fastball as soon as I got home. Grandma Marie had spent the night in the guest room and I should have known something was up. No sooner had I sat down at the table when they hit me with the bad news.

"Mikey, Grandma and I have decided you're going to have

to turn the cards over to us immediately."

It was like a punch in the gut. Sure, I knew they were talking about a trust fund and everything—but to actually give up my cards! It was like stealing my dog, that is if I'd had a dog to steal.

"Mom, you can't be serious!"

My mother and grandmother sat down beside me.

"Mikey, we can't go on spending money the way we did yesterday. I'm not going to let you blow it all on sunglasses and shoes. We have to think about your college education."

I was totally stunned.

"Mom, those are *my* cards."

"I know they are."

"Dad left them to me."

"I know he did."

"You can't take them away from me."

Grandma Marie put her wrinkled hand over mine.

"They're going into a safety deposit box this morning, Grandson, and that's all there is to it."

"All of them?" I asked in dismay

"I'm afraid so."

Suddenly I had the urge to dash to my room and stash a few Rizzutos for a rainy day. But my mother was wise enough to read my eyes.

"Don't even think about it, buddy."

"But, Mom..."

Both of them watched me like a hawk until it was time to go to the bank. I was never alone with my cards again. My mother locked them in her brief case and I didn't see them again until they were being loaded into a steel wall.

"Mom, I quit my route! What am I going to do for cash?"

"We're going to auction the cards like you said. But this is an adult business."

"I think you're being real unfair about this whole thing," I said.

"Mikey, you're still in control of them. You'll be the one who decides what you want to sell. Once we have the money we'll put you on a generous allowance.

I was outraged.

"An allowance! Mom, I own over $250,000 worth of cards. I don't want an allowance! I want my Mickey Mantles!"

I was making a scene in the bank and my mother glared at me.

"You keep acting like that and we'll cut you out of the deal completely. You won't see a cent until you're twenty-one. You want to start lugging newspapers again?"

That shut me up. But I was so mad I could have screamed. How could my own flesh and blood destroy my dreams? Somehow I was going to get those cards back.

Chapter Twelve

I spent the rest of the day in my room looking through the Yellow Pages for an attorney. I figured I'd sue my mother and force her to give me back the cards. I didn't know much about the law—but I knew I'd been robbed. There was this real empty space under my bed where my cards had been. Why hadn't I seen this coming and stashed a Pafko or two? At least I'd have a few thousand bucks. Now I had zip. When I finally left my room for lunch, I heard Grandma Marie talking to some auction house in San Francisco.

"So you need the cards by Friday if we want to be included in your next catalogue? Okay, I think we can arrange that."

I sat down at the table and stared at my smoked turkey and cream cheese sandwich. Did my mother actually think she could buy me off with great lunches? My grandmother hung up the phone.

"We're in luck," she announced. "Wolffers Auction House in San Francisco is just now finishing up their catalogue for their July auction. They're the ones who got $62,000 for the '52 Topps Mantle."

I stared at my grandmother over the rims of my shades. She sure was learning the baseball card business in a hurry. I took a bite of my sandwich. It was awesome.

"And the gentleman on the phone assures me," my grandmother continued, "that the Mantle they sold was slightly off center top to bottom. He seemed very impressed when I told him we had a gem mint example."

"You told him we only had one?" I asked with my mouth full.

Grandma Marie leaned back in her chair.

"Well, I didn't lie to the man. I simply neglected to tell him how many we had. No sense glutting the market, right Mikey?"

I gave her a surprised look.

"Grandma, don't tell me you're *actually* asking for my opinion?"

"Mikey—take off those sunglasses when you speak to your grandmother."

I removed the Ray Bans.

"And quit being a sarcastic brat."

"Yes, mother."

"Now tell us what you think we should sell first."

I shrugged.

"I don't really care."

"Mikey, don't act like that. We need your help."

I took an enormous bite of potato salad. It was more than my mouth could handle and it started oozing out from my lips.

"Stop that!"

I swallowed.

"If you want my help it's going to cost you 10 percent of the action," I said flatly"

"But that could be thousands and thousands of dollars. What do you need that kind of money for?" my grandmother asked.

I wiped my mouth with a paper towel.

"I want to go to baseball camp this summer so I can learn to hit Butch Wadski. I'm sick and tired of swinging at air."

My mother and grandmother looked relieved at my wholesome dream.

"Well, how much does that cost?" my mother asked.

"I'm not real sure, but I can find out. Chad Steele goes every year. That's why he can hit."

Grandma Marie smiled.

"Grandson, I think that would be money well spent."

"You do?" I asked in surprise.

"Yes, I do. A boy needs confidence in this world."

"I agree," my mother said.

"Wow, that's great."

"Now about the cards," my grandmother began.

I nodded.

"I think it's smart to sell the Mantles one at a time, Grandma. If the card they sold at auction was really off center and they got $62,000 for it—we should really clean up. I mean, two of ours are killer."

"And that's good?" my grandmother asked.

"Absolutely. I bet we can get $80,000."

"Do you think we should sell anything else?"

"Yeah, we've got to hype our find."

My mother and grandmother looked confused.

"What does that mean?"

"Well, in the card industry great discoveries of old cards are called finds. Sometimes these finds become legendary. I've read about the Paris Tennessee find by Alan Rosen. And some guy recently made a big find in Canada. When cards are part of a find it gets the buyers interested. We've got to create the Kenwood Find. And to make it exciting we're going to have to sell off some big stars in mint condition. I think we should sell a '52 and a '53 Mantle. Maybe a '52 Mays and Mathews. And about twenty other major cards."

Grandma Marie looked impressed.

"Mikey, it sounds to me like you've got the matter well in hand. Do you know anything about reserves?"

"Not really."

"The man on the phone just now wanted to know what kind of reserve we wanted to put on the Mantle."

"I think that means the lowest price we'll take for it," my mother said.

I nodded.

"That sounds right, Mom. I definitely think we should go for a new record. I think we should get at least $65,000."

My grandmother wrote this down.

"What about the other cards?"

"I think double book would be fair."

"Okay, fine. Looks like we've got some work to do, Grandson. The auction house wants the cards no later than

Friday. We have to bring them down in person so they can inspect them."

"Can of corn, Grannie."

"Can of what?"

"It means no problem."

"Oh, I see..."

Chapter Thirteen

The urge to slip a Berra down my pants was pretty strong as I sat in the safety deposit box room and sorted through my cards. But there was no way my mother and grandmother were going to let me get away with that. To tell you the truth, it was sort of a strange feeling to know your own mother doesn't trust you all that much. She and grandma were watching me like I was some sort of criminal as I made my choices.

"I think this '52 Mantle is the best one. I can't find anything wrong with it at all."

"Good."

"And this '53 Mantle is pretty incredible."

Both cards were placed in plexi-glass. Once they were encased they seemed to glow in the light of the vault. Not that I really had much time to admire them. Before I knew it they'd disappeared into the briefcase.

"I guess we can also sell one of these '57 Mantles."

"How many of those do you have?" my mother asked.

"Four, but this one has the best gloss."

"Okay."

I also picked out a Mathews' rookie, a '52 Jackie Robinson from the same series, a Willie Mays, an Andy Pafko that was so blazing it took my breath away, a Hoyt Wilhelm rookie, A '53 Mays, A '53 Satchel Page, and last but not least a dozen semi-stars in gem mint condition from the 1952 set.

"That should be enough for now."

"Good work, Grandson."

My stomach sank as I watched the rest of my cards slide back into the safety deposit box. My mother returned the metal drawer into the wall and turned the key. I've got to tell you it was painful to have all that money just out of my reach. If only I could get my hands on a Dickey, I'd be satisfied for a while.

"Mikey, don't look so sad. You're going to make a fortune."

"Yeah, right, Mom."

We left the bank in silence.

"So what'd you think these cards are worth?" my mother asked as she stared down at the briefcase in my grandmother's lap. She was at the wheel of the Explorer and headed for home. I sat in the back seat going over a list. Our appointment with the auction house was set for first thing the next morning.

"Well..." I began, "...if we get $65,000 for the '52 Mantle, and a 150 percent of *Beckett* for the rest...I figure we should take in a little more than a $100,000 for this first batch."

My mother looked stunned.

"But, Mikey, you hardly took any cards at all."

"I took the best of them, Mom."

"But we still have a pair of '52 Mantles, right?"

"That's right."

My mother beamed.

"This is getting pretty exciting."

She had that right.

Chapter Fourteen

I've got to give Chad Steele a lot of credit. Most guys would have said something crude about the fact that their sandwich wasn't the same old peanut butter and jelly—but not Chad. He ate his lox and cream cheese on a bagel like it was nothing new.

"So, Chad, I understand you're going to baseball camp again this year?" my grandmother asked as she refilled my friend's glass with milk.

"That's true, Mrs. Morris."

"Where are they holding it?"

"Cal State Hayward."

"Oh, really, when does it start?"

"I'm going in the second week of July."

"Do you think there might be anymore openings?"

Chad looked over at me with a funny expression.

"I'm not sure," he said after a moment. "Joe Morgan is going to be there this year, and he's real popular with the kids."

"I see. How much does it cost to attend?"

Chad swallowed a bite of his sandwich and blushed.

"Around four hundred dollars," he whispered.

Grandma Marie smiled.

"How would you like Mikey to go along with you this year, Chad?"

He grinned at me.

"That would be real cool, Mrs. Morris."

"I was hoping you could show him the ropes."

"No problem."

Later when we were finished with lunch, Chad and I went out into the back yard to play some catch. He had a smooth motion that sent the ball whipping across the grass and into my glove with a stinging pop

"So, Mikey, where'd you get the Ray Bans?"

"At the mall."

"You look real cool in them."

"Thanks," I smiled.

The ball went back and forth for a while.

"I guess you're wondering where I got the money for them, and where I'm getting the money for baseball camp, right?" I said after a few more tosses.

Chad shrugged.

"Well...you never went before."

I motioned for us to stop playing catch and we flopped down on the grass. Chad sat right next to me and we began to pound our mitts.

"I'll tell you something—but you've got to swear not to tell anyone else," I said with an air of mystery.

Chad leaned closer to me. I could smell the salmon on his breath.

"Mikey, you know you can trust me."

This was true. Chad knew how to keep his mouth shut. After all, he never told his sister how much I liked her.

"My father left me a bunch of old baseball cards."

Chad looked a little disappointed.

"Really. That's neat."

"Yeah, and they're all totally mint."

"Are they worth a lot of money?"

I smiled. Chad wasn't all that into baseball cards.

"They might be worth over $250,000," I said casually.

Chad's jaw dropped.

"Mikey, that's awesome. Can I see them?"

I shook my head.

"Naw, not right now, I've got them in a safety deposit box."

Chad frowned. He knew right away what had happened.

"You mean they didn't even let you keep one?"

I slammed the ball into my mitt.

"Nope," I admitted.

"But they're yours, right?"

"Oh, sure."

"And you don't want me to tell anybody about them?"

"Not right now. You can tell anybody you want after the auction."

"The auction?" Chad repeated.

"We're selling a bunch of them in San Francisco in six weeks."

"Cool. Are you going to quit your route?"

"I already did. I've got five more days and then I can sleep as late as I want."

Chad fell back on the grass and looked up at the sky.

"It's going to be great having you at camp this year. You'll really learn something."

I could feel a Will Clark game face spreading over my features.

"I just want to learn how to smash one of Butch Wadski's fastballs out of the park. I want it so bad I'd give a mint Berra for one home run. I'm getting sick and tired of striking out."

Chad grinned.

"Hey, Mikey, if Joe Morgan can't help you hit, then who can?"

I adjusted my Ray Bans.

"Yeah, I guess you're right. Want to go over to the park and hit a few?"

"Sure."

Chapter Fifteen

You might say I was the Cal Ripken of paper boys. As you may already know, Cal has played in more consecutive games than any other active player. The man always shows up for work. And that's how I was. It's pretty amazing when you stop and think about it. For over one thousand mornings in a row I dragged myself out of bed before dawn and hauled the news. I walked through pouring rain, I leaned into howling winds, and I saw some of the greatest sun rises that you can imagine.

All before the rest of you were even out of bed.

But I've got to be honest with you. I don't miss it. The idea of sleeping until I woke up naturally was my idea of heaven. I don't know if scientists have ever studied the matter—but I think the ringing of an alarm clock first thing in the morning might have a pretty major effect on a kid's brain. Sometimes it really scared me. Especially if I was having this great dream and all of a sudden this horrible sound invades my ears and gets right down inside my head. You sort of get used to it, but not really, if you know what I mean.

Anyway, during my last week on the route I began to have a lot of trouble concentrating on where Josh was suppose to be throwing the papers. We got three complaints in one day and I could tell Frank thought I was flaking out. But I just couldn't stop thinking about the auction and what I was going to do in baseball camp.

Grandma Marie had set everything up and I was really

going with Chad to Hayward. To tell you the truth, it was about the most exciting time of my whole life. All at once my blessings were rolling in like waves at the beach.

Imagine me and Joe Morgan standing around home plate discussing my swing. Man, that's the kind of experience that could really give a guy like me confidence.

But deep down inside I was getting a little nervous about the whole thing. What if my cards didn't sell? And what if even a Hall of Famer like Joe Morgan couldn't teach me how to hit Butch Wadski? Then where would I be? I began to see there was a lot of pressure on you when all your dreams start coming true. I also began to see that this summer was going to be a turning point in my life. Now that I was going to baseball camp, I wouldn't have anymore excuses if I blew it.

I was about to get my shot.

Chapter Sixteen

San Francisco scares me. It's only about an hour south of Kenwood—but it may as well be another planet for all I knew. On the trip to the auction house my stomach was gurgling with fear. What if I'd somehow misgraded my cards? What if the big city auctioneer laughed in my face? I kept telling myself that it wasn't going to happen. Hey--mint was mint! But what if I'd over-looked some micro defect on the '52 Mantle. After all, there was a million things that could go wrong with a baseball card. What if it was painted? Or trimmed! Or even fake!

Wolffers Auction House was on Kearny in a canyon of buildings that blocked out the sun. But I was shivering more from terror than the cold as we took the elevator to the fourth floor. Grandma Marie had made an appointment with a man named Harrison. As we were ushered into his office I felt like fainting.

"Good afternoon," Mr. Harrison said as he got out of his big leather chair. He was a handsome man with silver hair, and he looked rich.

My grandmother didn't waste any time with small talk. She placed the briefcase on Mr. Harrison's desk and snapped it open. I sat down in a corner chair and stared at the floor. Grandma Marie took out the '52 Topps Mantle and handed it to the auctioneer. Mr. Harrison took a quick look and then smiled.

"Well, well, this is indeed nice."

"You seem surprised, Mr. Harrison," my mother replied.

"Oh, I am, Mrs Morris, I am. You see, I get phone calls like yours all the time. You have no idea how many people call me claiming to have mint cards, when all they really have are reproductions or junk."

I squirmed in my chair.

"I hope you don't mind, but I'm going to have to take the card out of the plexi holder," Harrison explained.

It wasn't the kind of question that needed an answer. We sat in silence as the auctioneer removed the card and began to look at it with one of those things jewelers use to look at diamonds. I knew under a glass like that the surface of a baseball card looks like the moon with colorful craters. If one of those craters wasn't exactly right then the value of the card fell like a bloop single.

Harrison checked the Mantle out for a long time. I could see him looking at the corners and then along the edges. I felt like I was going to wet my pants as he got out a micrometer and measured card size and centering. A millimeter here or there could cost us thousands. Even Grandma Marie was beginning to look nervous. Finally Mr. Harrison turned off his powerful light and replaced the card in the plexi holder.

"This card is gem mint and will be advertised as such in our catalogue," he said.

"All right!" I whispered.

"I've never seen a '52 Mantle this nice before," he added.

Grandma Marie cleared her throat.

"What would be a fair reserve?" she asked

Mr. Harrison thought this over.

"Well, as you may know we got $62,000 for one that wasn't this nice about a year ago. But the market is very weak at the moment. Money is tight."

"Well...what would you suggest?"

"You may get only $50,000 for it."

I frowned.

"I want at least $65,000," I said firmly.

Mr. Harrison looked at me.

"I can't promise you that kind of bid."

I folded my arms over my chest.

"The reserve is $65,000, Mr. Harrison," I repeated.

"Okay, we'll give it a shot. You might get $100,000 for all I know. This is truly a great card."

"Fine," Grandma Marie interrupted, "now what about the rest of them?"

We sat in Harrison's office for almost three hours as he went over the rest of the of the cards. Most all of them got a mint grade. When we totalled up the reserves the figure came to more than $100,000.

"That's quite a number," my mother grinned.

I stood up.

"Mr. Harrison, I'd like you to list these cards as coming from the Kenwood Find."

The auctioneer smiled at me.

"Well, Mikey, twenty cards is usually not enough to be considered a find."

I returned his smile.

"We've got more cards, Mr. Harrison."

"You do?"

"Yes."

"More '52 Topps Mantles?"

I hesitated.

"Maybe," I admitted.

Mr. Harrison got to his feet and shook my hand.

"Well, in that case, Mr. Morris, I'd be very happy to list these cards as coming from the Kenwood Find."

"Thank you, sir."

"Thank *you*, young man."

We left with a receipt and color photocopies of all the cards that were going to be auctioned. I was walking on air as we headed back to the Explorer. Now all we had to do was wait for the cash to start rolling in.

Chapter Seventeen

On the first morning of my retirement I woke up at dawn and had my pants half way on before I realized I wasn't a paper boy anymore. Once my head cleared I hopped back into bed and slept 'til ten o'clock. Man, it was great. My whole outlook on life changed right away. Suddenly the future looked bright.

Even my mother seemed different.

She'd decided not to teach summer school like she usually did and had already quit all of her house cleaning jobs. Naturally, this gave us more time to spend together. We went to some baseball games in Oakland and even spent a week at Disneyland. Hanging out with my mom was really something special. She seemed more like an older sister than a mother. She had this new haircut and Ray Bans of her own and was looking real young and attractive.

But there was more to it than just a new look.

She seemed more relaxed. Before we found the cards she always had this kind of sad look in her eyes. Now they shined with happiness behind her sunglasses.

I think the Ford Explorer had a lot to do with us getting out more. When we had the Pinto it was no fun to go anywhere. We always had to worry about it blowing up or something. I can still see my mother hunched over the wheel of that wreck with a haunted look on her face as she stared at the warning lights. Was the heap going to boil over again? Was the battery going to die? Or worse yet—was it going to be us who died in some fiery explosion?

It was the kind of thing that could spoil an outing.

But all that car drama was history now. We were cool as we sat above the rest of the world in air conditioned comfort. Sometimes we'd just drive around with no particular place to go and listen to our favorite CDs. If we felt like it we'd stop in Napa and have some lunch. One day we even went hot air ballooning. It cost us a lot of money—but it didn't seem to matter anymore.

We were rich!

And we started talking about things we'd never talked about before. We even talked about Dad.

"Do you miss him, Mom?"

"Yeah, Mikey, I do. It's been over ten years since he died and I still dream about him all the time."

"I wish I could have known him better."

My mother and I were sitting in a restaurant in Sonoma. She suddenly leaned over and gave me a hug.

"I wish you could have known him better, too. He was a great guy. Always made me laugh. For a long time I was so mad at him for dying and leaving us alone. I've never told you this before, Mikey, but sometimes I found myself blaming him because our life was so hard."

My mother took a bite of her salad.

"It's funny," she continued, "the way things turned out. He's been dead for all these years and out of the blue he comes through for us. This whole thing with the baseball cards has taught me some lessons."

I opened my sandwich and peered at the ham.

"Like what?" I asked.

"Well, like life is strange. You never really know what's going to happen. It's kind of scary—but then again it's pretty exciting. I made a decision a few weeks ago. From now on I'm going to cut back on the worrying and enjoy life more."

I grinned.

"Me too, Mom. After all, once I'm in the big show you'll be sitting on easy street."

"The Big Show?"

"The Major Leagues, Mom, The Major Leagues!"

My mother and I looked at each other through our Ray

Bans and began to laugh.

"Mikey, you're really amazing."

"Hey--you've just got to believe in the magic," I said as I took a sip of my cherry Coke.

My mother smiled.

"I'm beginning to understand that, buddy."

Chapter Eighteen

I was pretty busy right after I found the cards so I missed a few of my Little League games. To tell you the truth, I really didn't feel like playing anymore until I'd had the chance to go to baseball camp. I was tired of being a strike-out artist—but after a week or so Chad talked me into showing up for a game against our old rivals the Hawks.

It was my one major mistake of the whole summer.

Thirty seconds after I got to the field Butch Wadski had his ugly face right into mine. He stood on his toes so we could be up close and personal. It was gross! His breath was actually fogging up my Ray Bans. But that wasn't the worst part—what really got my attention was the fact that he was standing on my new Nikes with his cleats. Butch could sense there was something different about me and he didn't like it.

"Where'd you get the fancy glasses, Morris?" he asked with a sneer.

"At the mall, Wadski."

"Yeah? Why don't you let me try them on?"

"No way."

Butch made a fist.

"Let me try them on, Morris, or I'll bash in your face."

People were beginning to stare. I wanted to shove Butch so bad my arms were shaking.

"Go ahead and push me, Mikey, I dare ya."

"Get off my toes."

"Make me, nerd."

I tried to squirm free but Wadski dug his toes into mine.

"What's the matter, Morris, are you going to cry?"

There was no way I was going to cry.

"You'd better leave me alone, Butch."

Wadski increased the pressure. Now I was sure he was causing some major damage.

"Hey, Morris, I hear you're going to some fancy baseball camp this year."

I frowned in pain.

"Who told you that?"

"My mother heard all about it at a school board meeting. What are you, rich?"

I curled my upper lip. Butch was surprised by my boldness but he hid it pretty well.

"Morris, you can go to all the baseball camps in the world and you're still not going to hit my fastball. Do you understand that? You're never ever going to hit one of my pitches!"

Wadski went for my sunglasses and the motion sent him back on his heels. I darted out from beneath his cleats and ran into our dugout.

"What was that all about?" Chad asked me as I sat on the bench.

I shrugged.

"I don't think Butch likes my new image."

"Forget about him."

Chad picked up a bat.

"I've got a feeling I'm going to smash one of his pitches out of the yard today."

I put my cleats on.

"I'd give a '52 Garagiola to do that," I said under my breath.

All the Garagiolas on the planet wouldn't have helped me much on that summer afternoon. I was swinging so bad it felt like the bat was made of lead. But it wasn't just me waving at air. Wadski was really on his game and mowed us down like the outfield grass. His fastball was hopping all over the place—but it always seemed to be in the strike zone. He was so good that day he didn't even bother to throw at us. He struck out twenty and walked only two. By the end of the game I had to admit that Butch was something special.

"Nice game, Ray Ban man," he grinned at me.

"You were great," I admitted.

Wadski shrugged.

"You just remember what I told you, Morris. Don't even think about hitting me."

There was a funny look in Butch's eyes and all at once I realized how serious he was about baseball. He'd rather kill you than let you get on base. As I walked off the field I began to wonder if I cared all that much. After all, it was just a game.

"Hey, Mikey," Chad called out to me. "Kelly and I are going over to Cafe Citti for a late lunch. You want to come along?"

All at once Kelly Steele was walking toward me from the third base side. She was wearing shorts and a sweat shirt that was about five sizes too big for her. Right away I felt like saying I was busy and running away—but then she smiled at me.

"Lunch sounds good," I heard myself say.

Kelly kept looking at me as we walked to the restaurant. It was the sort of glance I'd never seen from her before. Like she just wanted to shamelessly stare at me but was too shy. It made me feel great and I almost forgot about my three strike-outs.

"So, Mikey, I hear you're going to baseball camp with Chad this year," Kelly said after we'd sat down with our food.

I looked at Chad.

"Boy, there are no secrets in this town."

Chad raised an eyebrow to let me know that we did have a secret. Kelly didn't know about the baseball cards. She caught the expression and looked at both of us suspiciously.

"Chad, what was that look for?"

"What look?"

"You know what look. The look that says you two do have some kind of secret."

Chad gave Kelly a hard stare. Since I don't have any baby sisters myself I was amazed at her reaction. All at once she dropped her eyes and looked at her plate. I was stunned but Chad seemed to take this submission for granted. After that Kelly got real quiet but she kept looking at me. When Chad went to the bathroom we just stared at each other without blinking. I couldn't take my eyes off her.

"Kelly..."

"Yes, Mikey?"

I felt my face turn red.

"Nothing," I stammered.

Kelly looked disappointed but smiled anyway.

Later when lunch was over and I was back in my room, I had this real funny feeling in my stomach. It was all twisted up in knots and I thought I might toss my lunch.

I guess maybe I was in love.

What a summer!

Chapter Nineteen

I was having my own personal June swoon as I marked off the days on my calendar. The auction was set to happen a week after I got back from baseball camp—but July seemed like it would never come. Chad and I practiced night and day and my mother said we reminded her of the ladies who cleaned their house before the housekeeper got there. I guess she meant that Chad and I were trying to be perfect before we even got to Cal Hayward.

But I wanted to make a good impression.

The thought of making a fool of myself in front of Joe Morgan and a bunch of college coaches wasn't my idea of a real good time.

And I *was* getting better.

Chad pitched to me for hours. He was no Butch Wadski—but he had a decent arm. The important thing was he had control over where he was throwing the ball. I trusted him enough to know he wasn't going to bean me. That meant I could hang in there and concentrate on hitting. It wasn't long before I started making good contact.

"Mikey, your swing is looking better."

I ripped two shots down the third base line and then tossed my batting helmet on the ground. It was a beautiful day and we had the field all to ourselves.

"Don't you love the smell of a baseball diamond?" I asked Chad as we collapsed on the infield.

"Yeah..."

I had something important I wanted to talk about but I didn't want it to come out sounding too important.

"Hey, Chad, does Kelly ever talk about me?"

Chad began to retie the knots on his mitt.

"She talks about you constantly, dude."

"Really?"

"She gets on the phone with Becky or Stacy and talks about you like your whole lives were already planned out."

"You're kidding?"

"I wish I was. I'm getting sick of hearing about what a cute smile you have."

"Kelly thinks I have a cute smile?"

"And your hair. Boy, does she love your hair."

My heart was beginning to jerk around in my chest.

"I like her hair too, Chad."

"I know this, Morris."

"You do?"

"The way you two look at each other is really kind of sickening, if you want to know the truth."

"It's that obvious?"

"It is to me."

I thought about what to say next.

"Well, how do you feel about it?"

Chad started to pound the pocket of his mitt.

"You mean, how do I feel about you having the hots for my sister?"

"*Chad!*"

""Relax, Mikey, I was just giving you a bad time. Actually, I think you and Kelly make a great couple."

I fell on my back and stared up at the sky. The idea of me and Kelly being an actual couple was almost more than I could imagine.

"So, what'd you think I should do?" I asked.

Chad shrugged.

"Why don't you ask her to go steady?"

I felt lightheaded.

"Are you serious?"

"Or at least take her out to a movie."

"You mean like on a date?"

"Yeah, sure, why not?"

"But I'm only twelve and she's eleven."

"So what. I date Leah."

"Sure, but Leah is thirteen."

"It was just a suggestion, Morris."

I began to bang my foot with my bat.

"So you wouldn't mind if I dated your sister?"

"Nope. I know you'll treat her right."

Treat her right! That was the understatement of the summer. I'd treat her like a goddess. I'd shower her with gifts. All at once I imagined myself showing up at our next game with Kelly Steele on my arm. Man, would that make Butch Wadski crazy or what?

Chapter Twenty

The Fourth of July was always a big deal in Kenwood. People came from all over the place to watch the geeks bash each others heads in at the famous pillow fights, and to generally make fools of themselves while they pretended to celebrate our nation's independence. But that year I sort of got in the mood. I almost felt like it was a personal Independence Day or something. Because on the sixth of July I was taking off to baseball camp. And believe it or not, this would be the first time in my whole life that I'd ever slept anywhere but Kenwood.

Hard to believe, huh?

But it's the truth. Like I told you before, I'd never missed a single day on my paper route in three whole years, and before that I was really too young to be out on my own.

So this was it.

Mikey Morris on the loose.

As if that wasn't exciting enough, right before I was ready to leave for Hayward the catalogue arrived from Wolffers Auction House. This thing was really something. A big glossy book with only one card featured on each page. As I stared at my '52 Mantle and read the description it began to look like some kind of priceless painting. The catalogue made the colors so bright I almost wanted to buy it myself.

I was going to be *so* rich!

But that was later. Right then I had to focus on baseball. I had my duffle bag packed a week in advance; it was stuffed with just about everything in my dresser. Every pair of socks and underpants I owned was crammed in there. Mom had insisted on driving me and Chad to Hayward and I didn't make a big deal out of it. I knew she was pretty freaked out about leaving me alone with strangers for a whole week. She kept on asking Chad a lot of questions and handing me emergency phone numbers to call in case my head fell off or something. I tried to stay cool behind my Ray Bans but she was beginning to get on my nerves. A guy doesn't like to be treated like a baby in front of his best friend. Especially when they're about to go to camp. She must have told me about a thousand times to be sure to wear my batting helmet.

"Mom, I'll wear it to lunch if it makes you feel any better."

"Mikey, this is serious."

"They take real good care of us, Mrs. Morris," Chad said with a smile.

"I'm sure they do."

Mom was still a nervous wreck when we got there and insisted on getting out of the Explorer to inspect the place before she left. Right away one of the coaches showed up and seemed more than willing to give us a tour. He told my mother that we'd be sleeping in the dorms and that drinking and drugs were strictly forbidden.

After about ten minutes I began to notice that my mother was hanging on every word this guy had to say. Chad nudged me in the side and winked.

"You see the way the coach and your mom are looking at each other?"

I punched him in the arm.

"What are you talking about, Steele?"

"Oh, nothing."

It was around that time that I took a real good look at this Coach Larsen. He sort of reminded me of an old Jose Canseco who had kept himself in pretty decent shape. My mother looked like a little kid standing next to him. And to tell you the truth, Chad was right, they were looking at each other funny.

By the time we got to the playing field I knew something weird was going on. My mother was laughing at everything the coach said, and he was grinning like he'd just hit a grand slam during the World Series.

"Well, I'm sure the boys will be fine with you, Coach Larson."

"You can call me Roger, Mrs. Morris."

"And you can call me Jennifer."

I couldn't believe my ears.

"I'll walk you back to the car, Jennifer. You guys go back to the dorm and get settled."

"Yes, sir."

My mother kissed me good-bye and then strolled off with the coach like it was the most natural thing in the world.

"Man, I think they fell in love at first sight," Chad said as we headed to the dorms.

"Quit talking like that, Steele!"

Chad had this way of flaring his nostrils when he thought he was saying something clever. It was one of the few things I couldn't stand about him.

"Can you imagine how good you'd hit if that guy was your father?"

I got him in a head lock.

"Don't gross me out!"

Chad was gasping for air.

"I'm telling you, Morris, they had that look."

I let him loose. This was no time to concern myself with my mother's love life. I had to focus on baseball! I had to become a ball player!

Chapter Twenty-One

Chad and I ended up sharing a dorm room and it was almost like having the brother I'd always wanted. The first night after dinner we watched an orientation video with all the other guys and then went to sleep. At least I *tried* to sleep. My mattress was different from the one I had at home and I couldn't get very comfortable. Every time I went to doze off I'd start thinking about what was going to happen in the morning and get all pumped up. I also had a thought or two about the way Coach Larson and my mother had been looking at each other.

Finally around midnight I fell asleep.

At camp everybody is suppose to get up at seven-thirty but I woke up at five and stared at the ceiling for two hours. Chad was snoring so loud in the bed next to me that the windows were rattling. But I didn't have the heart to wake him up. At seven he opened his eyes and looked around in confusion. When he finally realized where he was he turned to me and yawned.

"Morning, Mikey, how'd you sleep?"

"Not that good. This mattress is too hard."

"You'll get used to it. Why don't we take a shower and then get our room ready for inspection?"

"Inspection?"

"Yeah, you're in the baseball army now, dude."

"Oh."

Taking showers with other guys was not something I was all that used to. You usually don't have to do that kind of stuff until you get to high school, but I was a ball player now, and everybody knows that ball players all shower together. Still, it was a shock seeing some of the older guys nude. They were all hairy and enormous in certain areas. Not that I was staring or anything, but sometimes a guy can't help but notice these kinds of things.

Anyway, after we got cleaned up and had our inspection we went to breakfast. We had our choice of tons of juices and different kinds of food. Like a fool I ended up drinking too much coffee and was twitching like Canseco by the time we started our warm ups.

"Mikey, do you always drink that much coffee?" Chad asked.

"Not always. I got in the habit doing my paper route."

After I ran around for about a half an hour I started to feel pretty normal. It was a perfect day for baseball and everybody was excited about getting started. We were all wearing our official camp T-shirts and hats so we sort of looked like a team. Once we got into tossing the ball around I could see that the coaches were checking us out.

A few hours later we were divided into groups according to our ages and how well we played. Somehow Chad and I ended up together. They started off by having us hit what they call an incredi-ball. It's this cloth covered thing that doesn't hurt even if it hits you in the head. The coach threw it right at us to help us get over our fear of the ball. I flinched once or twice, but pretty soon I was hanging in there with the best of them.

By lunch time I was pumped up.

"Wow, this camp is really cool," I said with my mouth full of tuna fish sandwich.

Chad grinned.

"Mikey, you haven't seen anything yet. Wait 'til we get to vision hitting."

I stopped chewing.

"What's vision hitting?" I asked.

"You wait, man. You're not going to believe your eyes."

Chad's words were still ringing in my ears as we headed back to the diamond. Coach Larson was fooling around with a pitching machine as we gathered around the plate. He motioned for us to step back out of the batter's box and all at once balls were flying over the plate like bullets.

"All right, gentlemen, listen up. I want you to keep your eye on the ball."

We watched them like snakes in the grass. After about three minutes the coach shut off the machine and came strolling into home like he was going to discuss something with a catcher who wasn't even there. He put his arm around Chad.

"What's you name, son?"

"Chad Steele, sir."

"Well, fellas, Mr. Steele here is the only one who understands the concept of vision hitting."

Everybody looked at Chad with admiration.

"And how do I know that?" the coach asked.

It was a good question.

"I know because Chad was the only one who followed the flight of the ball all the way to the back stop. The rest of you watched it 'til it crossed home plate and then turned your heads back to the mound."

We all stared at our cleats.

The coach smiled and motioned for us to sit on the infield grass.

"Fellas, what I'm going to teach you this afternoon will change the way you see the world. I'm going to open your eyes."

That sounded good to me.

"From now on you're going to see the baseball, gentlemen. Most of you are in soft focus at the moment. You're seeing too much when you watch a pitch. I'm going to teach you how to fine tune your eyes so that you block out everything but the ball. I want you to track it right into the catcher's mitt like Rickey Henderson. Once you get focused the ball will look much larger than it does now. It should also appear to slow down. Just a matter of concentration, gentlemen."

Was that cool, or what?

Coach Larson went back out to the mound and stood behind a mesh fence. He turned on the pitching machine and told Chad to step into the box. For the first time I noticed how he really did focus his attention on the ball. My old buddy had been keeping a secret from me. When it was my turn to bat I felt my knees start to knock like always.

"Hey, Mikey," the coach shouted, "we're here to have fun so relax and focus on the ball. Pick it up as soon as it comes out of the machine and track it. Don't even blink. Just see the ball and hit it."

I took a deep breath and calmed down. A few pitches went by and I watched them all the way to the backstop.

"That's it—now swing."

All at once the ball started looking like a slow moving cantaloupe. I took a cut and drilled one to left field. I got the barrel of the bat right on the ball.

"Way to hit, Morris. Now move back two inches in the box so you can get your arms fully extended."

I did what I was told.

My next swing was from the heels and I whiffed at air.

"Don't try and kill, Mikey. Okay, Jimmy, you're up."

I stepped out of the box and tried to keep my cool but my senses were on fire.

"Chad, I've never seen the ball like that before."

"No talking," the coach shouted.

I nodded and looked at Chad. He was watching every pitch even though he wasn't up. I started doing the same thing. It was incredible. I could see the seams on the ball!

Chapter Twenty-Two

I was totally focused on baseball camp when something happened that completely shattered my concentration. I was hitting off the pitching machine while Coach Larson watched when all of a sudden he started looking over my head into the stands behind me. When I stepped out of the batter's box to see what he was staring at, I couldn't believe my eyes.

It was my mother!

I frowned at her and then got back up to the plate. I ripped the next three pitches down the third base line and was ready for more when the coach stopped the machine.

"Okay, Mikey, that's enough for now."

"Coach, I'm in a groove!"

"You're finished for now, buddy."

"Yes, sir."

I walked back into the stands and gave my mother a half-hearted hug.

"Mikey, your hitting looks great."

"Thanks, Mom. Now why don't you tell me what you're doing here? Camp isn't over for another two days."

My mother looked over my shoulder. Coach Larson was coming toward us lugging a canvas bag filled with balls. The sun was low and he was casting a very long shadow. I guess he heard my question because he was the one who answered it.

"Your mother and I are going to dinner tonight, Mikey."

I was totally stunned.

"Huh?"

"I hope you don't mind, Mikey?" my mother said.

"Mind? Me? Why should I mind?"

Coach Larson smiled.

"Why don't you two have a nice visit while I get showered and ready to go?"

"Yeah, okay, Coach."

My mother and I began to walk across the grass to the dorms. The air was perfectly still and in the distance I could hear the sound of baseball chatter.

"Mikey," my mother began.

"Mom, I can't believe you're doing this to me."

"I'm not doing anything to you."

"You're dating the coach!"

"So?"

"So! I'm trying to concentrate on baseball here! I don't need the coach falling in love with my mother. You know how guys can be. If they find out they'll torture me."

"But you said you didn't mind."

"I was lying."

"Well, I'm not going to cancel dinner."

"Geez, I can't believe this. When did he ask you out?"

"The first day when he walked me back to the car."

"Mom, you hardly know this guy."

My mother smiled.

"That's why I'm going out with him. To get to know him better."

I stopped walking.

"Do you think this could be serious?" I asked.

"I don't know yet, Mikey."

"Me and Chad noticed right away how you two looked at each other."

My mother put her arm around me.

"You don't miss much, do you?"

I shrugged and decided to change the subject.

"Did you see how I was hitting the ball?"

My mother beamed.

"Are you kidding? I couldn't believe my eyes. I've never seen you swing like that before."

My chest swelled with pride.

"The coach has really been working with me."

My mother raised an eyebrow.

"More than he works with the other boys?"

"Yeah, now that you mention it. I guess he has."

"So, you really like Roger, huh?"

I nodded.

"I like him a lot. He's an incredible guy. He played third base at Stanford and was even in the Giants farm system for a while."

"He's not bad looking, either," my mother said with a wink.

"Mom, quit talking like that!"

My mother grabbed me and began to tickle my stomach.

"What's the matter, Mikey? Are you and Kelly Steele the only ones who can find each other attractive?"

"What?"

"I know you like her."

I squirmed free and began to run circles around her.

"I never said I liked Kelly Steele."

"Are you denying it?"

I grinned.

"Mom, you're just trying to change the subject."

She began to chase me.

"Hey, I'm not changing the subject. I thought we were talking about *LOVE!*"

My mother began to sing like one of those lame heavy metal bands from the last century.

"TALKING ABOUT LOVE!"

"Mom!"

"LLLLLLLOOOOOOOOOOVVVVVVVVVEEEEEE!

I tackled her and we fell to the grass.

"Mikey, you're ruining my dress!"

"You're the one in love, not me," I shouted.

My mother went limp and stared up at the sky. It was all purple and pink.

"You know what, Mikey?"

"No, what?"

"You may be right."

I fell into my mother's arms.

"But how can it happen so fast?" I asked.

My mother squeezed me.

"Beats me, kid. But have you taken a good look at Larson's body?"

I put my hand over my mother's mouth and quickly looked around to see if anyone was close enough to hear her.

"Mom, I can't believe you'd say something that..."

"That what?"

"That...crude!"

"Mikey, lighten up. Try and relax."

"Relax! My mother is hot for my coach and you want me to relax? This is the kind of thing that could set my career back a few summers."

She grinned her floppy grin.

"Yeah, maybe. But on the other hand it might be the best thing that ever happened to you."

Chad's words suddenly ran in my ears.

"...can you imagine how good you'd hit if a guy like that was your father..."

Chapter Twenty-Three

The next morning while I was doing my push ups I checked out the coach real close. He didn't look any different but now I was seeing him in a whole new light. I'd been in bed when they got back from dinner and had no idea what they'd been doing all night. I couldn't help but wonder if Coach Larson had kissed my mother.

"Hey, Mikey, go all the way down!"

I touched my chin to the grass and then pumped myself back up. Later that morning my hitting was pretty good but I still had mom and the coach on my mind so I decided to call home.

"Hi, Mom, it's me."

"How's it going?"

"Not bad. How was your date?"

"It was great."

"Did you kiss him?"

"Mikey!"

"I've got to know."

"Well...yes, I did."

"On the lips?"

"Yes."

"Geez. Are you going to see him again?"

"As a matter of fact, I'll be coming down on the last day of camp to have dinner with you."

I didn't say anything.

"Mikey, are you still there?"

"Yeah, I'm here."

"Is everything okay?"

"Oh, sure."

"What's wrong?"

"I think I'm scared or something."

"Scared of what?"

"Scared that Coach Larson might be my new father."

"Mikey, we've only had one date."

"I know, but it seems different somehow."

"I think you're right about that."

"And I just don't want to start thinking about him like that and then be disappointed."

My mother took a sharp breath.

"Oh, Mikey..."

"What?"

"I know how much a boy needs a father."

This was shaky ground.

"Mom, it hasn't been that bad."

All at once my mother was sobbing.

"Yes, it has! We've just never admitted it to each other before. Seeing you at baseball camp with Roger has shown me how much you thrive on a little male attention."

I knew she was right.

"So you really like Roger?" she asked me.

"Yes."

My mother was sniffling.

"Maybe things will work out."

"Don't press, Mom."

"What?"

"Don't push it."

"Oh..."

"Just have fun."

"Is that what they teach you at camp?"

"One of the things."

"Sounds like good advice."

"Old baseball wisdom, Mom."

"It's really more than a game, isn't it?"

"Mom, it's my life!"

Chapter Twenty-Four

Joe Morgan himself showed up on the last day of camp and stood around home plate signing autographs and talking about baseball. Just having a Hall of Famer on the diamond with you was a special kind of feeling—but I was so surprised you could have picked me off first when he actually came over to talk to me while I was taking my swings.

"What's your name, son?"

"Mikey Morris, Mr. Morgan."

"You've got a nice looking swing."

I grinned like a fool.

"And fast hands."

"Thank you."

A moment later Morgan turned away from me to talk to another kid—but I knew from now on I would always have a nice swing and quick hands. No one was ever going to tell me different. All at once I had a positive self-image that I could take with me every time I went to the plate. I hit a few more and then let someone else take my place. Joe was handing out baseball blessings like a priest. This guy knew secrets most of us only dream about.

After all, he'd been in the big show.

"What'd he say to you, Mikey?" Coach Larson asked.

I smiled.

"He said I had a nice swing and fast hands."

The coach nodded.

"He's right. You've got the tools."

Talk about an amazing week! Six days ago I was a hitless geek with the confidence of a worm. Now all of a sudden I couldn't wait to face Butch Wadski and his wild fastball.

"Hey, coach," I said as people began to file off for dinner. "Why don't you throw me a few heaters?"

"Now, Mikey..."

"I can hit them."

"Mikey, I'm a full grown man."

"Just give me a chance."

"I admire your confidence, fella, but I don't want to destroy it."

"Okay, okay, then just throw it as fast as the fastest twelve year old.

Coach Larson nodded.

"Ten pitches and then we go to dinner."

"Great."

I got in the batter's box. The coach started pumping them in there. I let two go by while I got into his rhythm. On the third pitch I took him long and deep.

"Nice hit, Mikey."

"Pitch faster."

The coach smiled and reared back to heave some smoke. It was right over the plate and I swung hard but the ball hopped up at the last second and I only got a piece of it. It flew back and slammed against the backstop.

"Mikey, I can't believe you even fouled that one. Your timing was almost perfect on my fastest heater."

I dropped my bat and looked up at the sky.

"I can hit!" I screamed.

Coach Larson walked toward the plate.

"Seeing you improve like this really makes me feel good."

"Makes *you* feel good! Can you imagine how I feel? I can't wait to get back to Kenwood and face Butch Wadski."

"Who's that?"

"He's a left hander for the Kenwood Hawks. The guy has been striking me out ever since I was nine. He's made me feel like a loser for a long time."

"Can Chad hit him?" the coach asked.

"Yeah, sometimes. He got a home run off him once."

"Then you can, too."

"You think I hit as good as Chad?"

"I think you could be better than Chad."

"Really?"

"It's all a matter of confidence. Once you take this Butch guy downtown a few times your attitude will change. Up 'til now he's owned you. Had your number. Once you show him you can hit off him he won't be so cocky. You've got to make him fear you. Earn his respect."

I looked up at the coach.

"Did I mention that Butch is about the meanest guy in my neighborhood and that he swore to bash in my face if I ever nailed one of his pitches?"

Coach Larson smiled.

"No, Mikey, you didn't mention that, but the world is full of Butch Wadski's. Hey, look at Joe Morgan. He's a little guy. But he never let anyone push him around. You think he got into the Hall Of Fame without a fight? Baseball is war."

"So, you think I'm going to have to fight Butch?"

"No, way. Just hit the ball."

"But what if he does punch me?"

"Then you're going to have to defend yourself."

The idea of fighting with Butch gave me a queasy stomach.

"Let's grab some dinner," the coach said.

I smiled.

"Anxious to see Mom?" I asked.

Coach Larson lifted me off my feet and spun me around.

"Yeah. You want to make something of it, Morris?"

The coach and I were laughing our heads off as we crossed the diamond. Suddenly I wasn't afraid of anything.

Chapter Twenty-Five

It wasn't all that bad seeing my mother sit next to the coach at dinner. She looked real happy with him, and none of the other guys teased me about it. In fact, I could tell that most of them were sort of impressed. Later that night as we drove home I began to wonder what it would be like to have Coach Larson around all the time. I knew I was going to miss the guy if things didn't work out between him and Mom, and I was getting a little nervous about how much he was starting to mean to me.

"Mom, do you and Roger have another date planned?" I asked as we headed north to Kenwood.

My mother smiled at me.

"Yeah, Mikey, we do. He'll be coming to the auction with us tomorrow night. He seems very interested in your cards."

"You told him about them?" I asked in dismay.

"Yes, I did. I hope you don't mind?"

I shrugged.

"No, I guess not. Actually, it'll be nice having the big lug around to protect us and help us carry all the money home."

"Mikey, don't call Roger a lug."

"Just kidding, Mom."

"And don't go getting your expectations up about this auction. We have no idea what's going to happen. Maybe no one will meet your reserves. After all, you are asking more for your Mantle than anyone has ever paid before."

It was getting dark so I took off my Ray Bans.

"The 'Mick' will sell, Mom."

"I hope you're right."

There was no doubt in my mind that I was right. Mikey Morris was on a hot streak. Nothing was going to go wrong. I was going to be rich. Just the thought of it made me shake with excitement. For the first time in my life I was going to be able to afford anything I wanted. I was going to have all the latest video games, and a bunch of new clothes.

"So, how is Grandma Marie doing?" I asked to keep my mind off all that cash.

"She's doing real well. I think she's as excited about this auction as you are."

"Has she met Roger?"

"No, not yet."

"Do you think she'll like him?"

"That's hard to say. Sometimes she has funny ideas about people. But I'm sure when she sees how much Roger means to both of us she'll come around."

I turned toward my mother.

"I wonder what it would be like for you to get married again after all these years. I mean, I can't remember having a man around the house. It's always been just you and me."

My mother frowned.

"Mikey, don't start moving too fast. I think marriage is the last thing on Roger's mind at this point. Taking on a woman with a child is a lot of responsibility..."

All at once I felt weird.

"Mom, do you think having me around is going to hurt your chances?"

"Oh, Mikey, I didn't mean it to sound like that. You know how much Roger likes you. He talks about you all the time. He says you made more progress at camp than anyone else."

I looked out the window.

"Maybe that's because I was so lame to begin with."

"Hey, what happened to all that confidence?"

I grinned as we entered the Valley of the Moon. The sight of the rolling hills covered in grape vines always made me feel better. And Mom was right. I was worrying too much.

Chapter Twenty-Six

The next night we arrived in San Francisco about an hour before the auction and went to a restaurant called Harry's. It was one of those hot dog places where you could get a seat next to the window and watch everybody walk by on the street. I sat next to Grandma Marie facing my mother and Coach Larson. Grandma was checking him out real close, but she waited until he had his mouth full of chili dog before she asked him anything.

"So, Roger, do you go to church?" she asked out of the blue.

The coach had his mouth stuffed, but he swallowed quickly and took a gulp of his root beer.

"Yes, Marie, I do."

"Might I ask what denomination?"

"I'm a Catholic."

Grandma Marie smiled a little.

"Well, that's nice."

Roger looked out the window like he wanted to talk about something else. A bunch of people were hustling by and most of them looked pretty weird.

"Mikey, do you think you can tell much about a person just by looking at them?" the coach asked me.

"What'd you mean?"

"See all those people out there?"

"Yeah."

"What can you tell me about them?"

I took a sip of my Coke.

"What'd you want to know?"

"Look at those two guys in double-breasted suits. What kind of work do you think they do?"

My grandmother spoke up before I got a chance.

"Looks to me like they work in a clothing store," she cracked. "They look like mannequins. No real man would be caught dead in a suit like that."

Roger pointed to a guy in a seersucker jacket.

"What about him?"

"A reporter," I said quickly and with confidence.

"Why do you say that?" my mother asked.

"Because he's got a tape recorder in his pocket," I replied.

Roger nodded.

"See what I mean? It's amazing how much you can tell about a person just by looking at him."

My mother turned to Roger.

"What do you see when you look at me?" she asked him.

I couldn't believe my ears and almost choked on my hot dog. Mom wasn't exactly beating around the bush. The coach gazed at her with this mushy kind of stare. I was afraid to look at my grandmother to see what she was thinking about all this so I just read the labels on the mustards. This place had about a hundred different kinds.

"I see goodness," Roger said.

It could have been a lot worse.

"I like that," my mother beamed.

But the game wasn't over.

"Now what do you see when you look at me?" Roger asked my mother.

"I see big!" I giggled.

"And I see sweet," my mother added.

Everyone turned to my grandmother.

"And I see that we're going to be late," she said as she glanced at her watch. "I think we'd better get to the auction."

That was fine with me. I didn't really want to know what everybody saw when they looked at me. I inhaled the rest of my hot dog and we walked across the street to Wolffers. The auction was set to begin a six o'clock and we wanted to get good seats.

As we got out of the elevator and stepped into a narrow hallway I was stunned to see so many people. Most of them were men dressed in old baseball jerseys and carrying expensive looking briefcases.

"Quite a turnout," my grandmother said.

A woman behind a small table signed us up and gave us a bidding card and another catalogue. There was still ten minutes to go before the auction got started and no one was allowed to enter the room early. Near the door there was a long table filled with soft drinks and cookies. I popped a Coke and leaned against the wall. Two seconds later the guy in the seersucker jacket that I'd seen on the street stuck a microphone right under my nose.

"Are you here to buy some cards, son?" he asked me.

"No, sir, I'm selling."

The man seemed impressed.

"Oh really? What are you offering?"

Grandma Marie was standing next to me so I looked over at her. She nodded like it was all right for me to talk about it.

"Well, I've got quite a bit actually. Everything in the Kenwood Find."

The reporter looked through his notes.

"So that would include the gem mint '52 Topps Mantle?"

"That's right."

People began to stare at me.

"That's quite some card."

"Yeah, it is."

All at once the crowd began to file into the auction room. Roger stepped between me and the reporter and gently shoved me toward the door.

"Hey, kid. Where'd you find the cards?"

I put on my Ray Bans.

"No further comment," I shouted.

"Nice touch, Mikey," my grandmother smiled as we took our seats.

Once we were seated I began to check out the room. Along one wall was a bunch of strange people whispering into phones. Most of them looked like punk rockers who had forced themselves into suits for the occasion. We were sitting in the second

row. Right in front of us were two television sets with real bad
color. Behind the TVs there was a stage with a podium like in
church. Now that I think about it the whole place reminded me
of church.

"Are you getting excited, Mikey?" my mother asked.

"I'm pumped, Mom."

A guy with a fancy candy apple red briefcase leaned over
from the row behind us and whispered in my ear. He had a wild
look in his eyes like maybe he hadn't slept much in the last
week.

"So you're the guy with the '52 Topps Mantle?"

I nodded and adjusted my sunglasses. This guy had a
funny accent and there was something scary about him. As he
leaned back in his chair, he snapped open his case and made
sure I saw that it was stuffed with hundred dollar bills.
Grandma Marie saw the money too and pulled me close.

"Everything is going to be fine, Mikey."

The auctioneer entered the room like he was some kind of
celebrity or something. He shook hands with a bunch of people
and called them by their first names. Then he got up behind the
podium and took a sip of his diet Coke.

"Okay, folks, listen up. We've got over thirteen hundred
lots to move tonight. So things are going to happen fast. Let's get
started with the Old Judge Tim Keefe. A real nice card and very
rare. The opening bid is $1,800. Who'll give me $2,000?
Anybody want to bid? No? Sold to the book for $1,800!"

"What does that mean?" I asked my mother.

"I don't know."

The guy with the cash leaned over.

"It means the card was sold to someone who made an
advance bid. No one on the floor or phones wanted to top it."

"Oh..."

I began to wonder if anyone had made an advance bid on
my '52 Mantle. I sat and watched the television screens as a
bunch of old tobacco cards flashed before my eyes. It was like
watching the entire history of baseball. Some of the old players
looked like gun fighters.

"I can't believe the money these people are spending," my
grandmother whispered as a Babe Ruth card went for $5,000 to

the guy sitting behind us. When the deal was done all his friends high fived him like he'd just hit a grand slam in the World Series. The Ruth card had sold for a little over a third of its estimate.

"Yeah, they're spending money," I said. "But things are going cheap."

"It's a recession, Mikey."

Before long we started getting to the more modern players. A nice Ted Williams from the forties went for $1,000. Once in a while the auctioneer would stop the action and tell a story about his favorite baseball players. It was a good thing because the auction was moving so fast it was making my head spin. I kept counting the pages of the catalogue to see how much further we had to go before we got to my first card. It was the '52 Topps Mays and I had high hopes for it.

Finally we reached it and I felt my mouth go dry.

"All right, here's lot 214. A gem mint '52 Topps Mays from the Kenwood Find. Perfectly centered, folks. This is the nicest one we've ever offered at Wolffers. Let's start at $2,000. I've got $2,000! I've got $2,500 on the phones. I've got $3,000 in the back. I've got $4,000 on the phones."

I began to hop in my chair.

"I've got $4,500 in the back. Everybody wants this card. Absolutely gem mint. A blazer! I've got $5,000 on the phone. The man is relentless. Who will give me $5,500?"

A silence fell over the room.

"Fair warning!"

No movement.

"Sold to the phone bidder for $5,000!"

"All right, Mikey," my mother squealed.

I was cranked up to the max. Five thousand for the Mays was more than I ever dreamed of. My Mathews, Robinson, and Pafko didn't do as well but they all sold for more than the reserve. Suddenly there was a break in the action and the auctioneer took a long drink of his Coke.

"And now ladies and gentlemen I offer you lot number 223. The '52 Topps Mickey Mantle. This is without question the finest example of number 311 that we've ever had the privilege of offering here at Wolffers. The card is perfectly centered with a dazzling gloss and has absolutely no flaws. I think you'll agree that it might well be the best of its kind. I have an opening bid of $45,000. I have $46,000 from the phones. I have $47,000 in the center of the room."

The guy with the fancy briefcase full of money had his bidding card up and his eyes on the ground.

"I have $48,000 from the phone."

The man behind us kept his card up.

"I have $49,000 from the center of the room."

Suddenly an awful silence came over the room.

"I have $49,000. Can I get $50,000?"

My stomach began to sink.

"Fair warning at $49,000."

No more bids were coming in. The auctioneer checked his notes and then said:

"No sale!"

The guy behind me leaned forward.

"I guess your reserve was too high, kid."

I felt stunned like I'd just watched a third strike go by. I looked at my mother and grandmother in confusion.

"I can't believe it," I mumbled.

"Maybe we should take a break," Roger suggested.

I nodded, but when I tried to stand my knees were too weak to hold me up. I had to lean on the coach to get out of the room. Once we were in the hall I felt like I was going to burst into tears.

"I can't understand it," I said as I took a cookie. "I thought the last Mantle like mine sold for $62,000."

"I guess the market has changed."

The guy with the briefcase full of money came over and stood next to me. He helped himself to a Coke and took a long gulp.

"How much was your reserve, kid?" he asked me with a leer.

I looked at my grandmother.

"Go ahead and tell him, Mikey."

"Sixty-five thousand," I whispered.

The guy with the briefcase let out a soft whistle.

"That's nuts," he said simply.

I turned to him.

"No it's not! A year ago they sold one that wasn't as nice as mine for $62,000."

"That was a year ago, buddy. People are beginning to think the '52 Topps Mantle is a little pricey. Why should it bring more than the '51 Bowman? That's Mantle's real rookie card. And why should it cost twenty times more than the Mays?. Sort of smacks of racism, wouldn't you say? Besides San Francisco is the wrong place to sell that card. You'd get more for it in New York where I'm from."

My shoulders slumped.

"Tell you what I'll do, kid. I'll give you $55,000 for it."

I turned to my grandmother.

"You mean after the auction?" she asked the man.

"No, I can't do something like that. I've got a relationship with these people. But after the auction everything that didn't sell can be had for one bid higher."

My grandmother shook her head.

"Not if that bid doesn't meet the reserve," she said flatly.

The man nodded.

"Yeah, that's true enough."

My grandmother took me aside.

"I think we should take $60,000 if we can get it," she advised.

"I think so too, Grandma."

"We'll take $60,000, young man."

The guy with the briefcase looked offended.

"No way, lady. You saw what happened in there. No one in the country was willing to pay even $50,000. I'd be giving you $10,000."

Grandma Marie leveled her eyes at the man.

"I know you want that card, fella. It's the best one you've ever seen, isn't it?"

"It's okay."

"Give us $58,000 and it's yours."

"I can't go over $55,000."

"Take it for $56,000."

"Okay, lady, $56,000 it is."

Grandma Marie shook the man's hand and we returned to

our seats. A bunch more of my cards had sold. My mother had stayed in the auction room to write down the numbers. As I went over them I felt better. Only the '52 Mantle had brought in less than I'd expected. The rest of the stuff was selling for top dollar. I began to add up the figures as the last of my cards was auctioned off. The total came to almost $90,000. Not bad, but I was still a little upset about my Mantle.

The auctioneer kept right on selling.

"And now we offer lot number 784. The finest home jersey we've ever had. A game worn Mickey Mantle from his rookie year. I have an opening bid of $100,000. Now I have $110,000. And $120,000 from the phones. There's $130,000 from the back of the room."

I couldn't believe the bidding. The recession didn't seem to have much effect on sportswear.

"My word," my grandmother mumbled. "Who would pay $150,000 for a used shirt?"

I had no idea.

After the auction was over the guy with the briefcase kept his word and bought my Mantle for $56,000 cash. All in all he'd spent about $400,000 in one night. The last I saw of my Mantle was when he placed it next to his new Babe Ruth and disappeared with his body guards. The auction house said it would have a check for me in a few days.

Chapter Twenty-Seven

A week later a check arrived for $81,000. The auction house had taken 10 percent right off the top for its services. It was a lot of money but I couldn't help but feel disappointed. My Mantle hadn't set any records and I knew it was one of the best in the nation. Roger and I were sitting in the park talking about it.

"Timing is everything, Mikey."

"Yeah, I guess so."

It was cool having someone like the coach around to clear up my thinking. Roger had been spending a lot of time with Mom and me, and when he told me something I listened.

"It's time to forget about the money and start thinking about how you're going to hit Butch Wadski. You've got a game this weekend against the Hawks, don't you?"

I nodded that I did.

"And who's going to be pitching?"

I smiled at the thought of Wadski.

"Butch," I said.

"And what are you going to do to him?"

I began to jerk my head around like Canseco. I jerked so hard my Ray Bans flew off my face and onto the ground.

"I'm going to crush him!"

"What did you say, buddy?"

"I said—I'M GOING TO SMOKE HIM!"

"You've got to believe it, Mikey."

"I do believe it!"

I put my sunglasses back on and flopped on the grass.

"But what if I don't?" I whispered.

"Don't what?"

"Don't crush him."

"Then you keep after him until you do. You make hitting Butch Wadski a mission."

I was so into what Roger was saying that I didn't even see Kelly Steele until she was practically standing on top of me. I jumped to my feet and began dusting off my butt like some kind of nerd.

"Kelly, I didn't see you."

Kelly extended her perfect hand to Roger.

"Hi, I'm Kelly Steele."

"Nice to meet you, Kelly. I'm Roger Larson."

"I know who you are, Coach. I'm Chad Steele's sister."

"Of course."

"Mikey and my brother are constantly talking about you."

"Well...that's very flattering."

Suddenly Kelly turned to me.

"Mikey, would you like to go over to the pizza place with me and have something to eat?"

I was speechless.

"You mean just the two of us?"

"Uh, huh."

Roger stood up.

"That sounds like a good idea, Mikey. I've got to get back to your place anyway. I promised your mother I'd mow the lawn. Have you got enough money?"

Kelly looked insulted.

"He doesn't need any money. I asked him so I'm treating."

Kelly Steele was actually going to buy me lunch!

"Well, okay then. Have a good time," Roger said.

Walking side by side with Kelly made me almost sick to my stomach with joy. About halfway to the pizza parlor she grabbed my hand and held it like it was the most natural thing in the world.

"So, I guess this is our first date, huh, Mikey?"

"Yeah, I guess so."

"I never want to forget this moment," Kelly said.

I knew I was never going to forget it.

As soon as we got to the pizza parlor I noticed something weird was going on. Everybody was staring at us with these stupid grins on their faces. Kelly was still holding my hand and when we sat down I asked her what she thought everybody was looking at.

"People like to watch young lovers," she said with a smile.

I almost choked on my ice.

"Is that what they think we are?"

Kelly stared into my eyes.

"I like you a lot, Mikey."

I felt myself blush.

"I like you too, Kelly."

A few minutes later the pizza arrived. Watching Kelly eat gooey cheese was about the most fascinating thing I'd ever seen. I loved her lips and the way her nostrils flared from the steam coming off the pizza. That afternoon I was the happiest guy in Kenwood.

Chapter Twenty-Eight

I guess love is pretty much the same no matter how old you are. So it was pretty easy for me to understand how Mom felt about Roger. Still, I've got to tell you that I was a little embarrassed when I saw them kissing and hugging around the house. It gave me a strange feeling. But I'd be lying if I told you I wasn't interested in how these things were done. Up 'til that summer I'd never kissed a girl on the lips, which made me kind of a retard in that area. In this day and age most guys have done a whole lot more than kiss by the time they're twelve.

But even though I was real curious I wasn't all that sure I wanted to talk about it with my mother.

"So, Mikey, did you have a good time with Kelly?" she asked me the next morning at breakfast.

"Yeah, sure, Mom."

"She seems to like you a lot."

"I like her too."

My mother cleared her throat. I couldn't bear to look at the expression on her face.

"You know, Mikey, love is a wonderful thing."

I started to butter my toast.

"Mom, are we going to talk about sex now?"

"Well..."

"I think I need to know a few things," I admitted.

My mother looked surprised.

"What would you like to know?" she asked me.

"Let's start with kissing."

My mother gave me her crooked smile. At least we were starting on safe ground.

"You're interested in kissing, Mikey?"

"I think Kelly expects it."

"But she's only eleven."

"Chad told me she's already kissed some guys."

"I see."

"Not a lot of guys. Just some guys."

"I understand."

"So, how do you do it?"

"Well, to tell you the truth, it's something you learn by doing. It's always a little awkward at first but you get the hang of it."

"Sounds like hitting."

"I guess so. Practice makes perfect."

"How do I know when to kiss her?"

"You'll know."

"You mean like it's a natural instinct?"

"You might say that."

I poured some milk on my cereal.

"What about the rest of it?" I asked.

"You mean sex?"

"Uh, huh."

"What have they taught you in school?"

"We've seen some films. Mostly they tell us not to do it."

"Do you know what *it* is?"

"Why don't you tell me?"

There's no way I'm going to write down what my mother said next. If you want to know about that kind of stuff you can ask your own mother or father. But I will say this much, it was a pretty strange conversation and made me see the world in a whole new way.

People do some strange things—even mothers.

The next day I went over to Kelly's house to go swimming and while we were splashing around in the pool it happened. I swam up to her underwater like I was a seal, and when I came to the surface we were face to face. Boy, was Mom ever right. One look into Kelly's eyes and those instincts really kicked into gear.

I knew this was the big moment so I leaned in close. Naturally I had no idea what I was doing, but when our lips met the hairs on the back of my neck started to tingle.

"Wow!

The whole thing didn't last that long and when it was over I slipped back down under the water to hide my excitement. I guess I did all right because Kelly swam after me and when we got together under the diving board she put her arms around me and everything.

"Kelly," I gasped.

"What?

"That was great."

"Yeah, not bad for your first time."

I was insulted.

"What makes you think it was my first time?" I asked.

Kelly gave me another kiss.

"A girl can tell."

I splashed her in the face and swam to the other end of the pool. The sight of her coming after me was almost more than I could bear.

Kelly was the one for me.

Chapter Twenty-Nine

Kelly was on my arm the next day when I showed up for our game against the Hawks. I could almost see the steam coming out of Butch Wadski's ears when he saw us together. I know he would have jumped me on the spot if Roger hadn't been with us. Instead he went to the mound and began throwing blazing fastballs at his terrified catcher.

"That boy does have a pretty good arm," Roger admitted as he watched Butch warm up.

"Yeah," I whispered.

"And he's a lefty."

"And *real* wild," I added. "I can never get comfortable in the batter's box because I'm always afraid that he's going to bean me."

Roger nodded.

"Does he throw at batters on purpose?"

I shrugged.

"No one knows for sure, but he hits a lot of guys."

Roger leaned forward and watched Butch real close. Finally he turned to me with a grin.

"You can hit him, Mikey."

"You think so?"

"I know so. I've thrown you much harder stuff."

"Yeah, but you throw it over the plate."

"You can't be afraid of him."

"That's easy to say, Coach."

I turned around and looked at Kelly and my Mom in the stands. They were giggling and for a moment I wondered what they were talking about. Was Kelly telling her about the kiss?

"Hey, Mikey, pay attention to the pitcher. Start focusing on him right now," Roger advised.

"Okay."

I turned my attention back to Wadski. I watched his motion and how he released the ball. Pretty soon everything I'd learned at camp started coming back to me. I was staring at Butch so hard he stopped pitching and came swaggering over to our dugout.

"What're you looking at, Morris?"

I held my ground.

"Your motion, Butchmeister."

Wadski couldn't believe my mouth. He glared at me with pure hatred. Roger had gone into the stands but he was still aware of what was going on.

"So, you're a wise guy now, huh, Morris?"

"You don't scare me anymore, Butch."

Wadski laughed to himself.

"Do you really think you can hit me now that you've gone to that fancy camp of yours?"

"I know I can hit you, Butch."

Wadski took a step in my direction.

"I guess you think you're a pretty big man having your arm around Kelly Steele, but let me tell you something, nerd. She won't like you nearly as much once I mess up your face with my slider. I'm going to destroy that mouth of yours."

"Is that the only way you can get me out, Butch?"

Wadski tensed and then spun around and headed back to the mound.

"Did you two have a nice chat?" Chad asked as I stepped into our dugout.

"Nothing important," I said as I put on my cleats.

Kelly leaned in from the stands.

"Are you going to hit a homer for me, Mikey?"

"Maybe."

Once the game got started my stomach really began to churn. I made one nice catch in the outfield but it didn't do all that much to stop the butterflies. When it was our turn to bat Butch struck out the side and then smiled at me as I ran back out to right field.

"Looks like I've really got my stuff today, Morris."

I gave him my Will Clark game face and trotted out to my position. I was still so nervous I could barely stand up. Nothing was hit to me but by the time I got back to our dugout I was having trouble breathing.

"Mikey, you look sort of pale."

"I'll be all right."

Frank Smith, our clean-up hitter was first up. I watched Butch pitch to him. Frank made a good effort but he didn't come close to hitting the ball. Wadski mowed him down with five pitches and then pumped his arm in the air. I moved from the dugout to the on deck circle as Chad stepped to the plate.

"Come on, Chad, you can do it," I chattered.

My friend got set as Butch glared in for a sign. The first pitch was an inside fastball that rose at the last second and barely missed hitting Chad in the head. I turned and looked at Roger and he gave me the stay cool sign.

"Way to watch them, Chad," I yelled.

Wadski threw the next three right down the middle with so much heat Chad didn't even move the bat off his shoulder. I looked down at the grass as he passed.

"Old Butch is a demon today, Mikey."

"Thanks for the encouragement," I said.

Butch was grinning from ear to ear as I stepped to the plate. I got set and he went into his windup. The first pitch was outside but he got the call anyway.

"Strike one!"

I turned and looked at the umpire.

"You got a problem, Morris?" he asked me.

"No, sir."

I stepped back in and tried to focus, but I couldn't seem to concentrate. The ball was rising and hopping all over the place.

"Strike two!"

I backed out of the batter's box and took a deep breath. Roger made a tunnel with his hands around his eyes. It was the signal to focus on the ball. I got into the batter's box again and began to wave my bat with as much menace as I could manage. The next offering was a curve and I actually got a bead on it. I waited until the last second and took a tremendous cut.

"Strike three!"

I missed it by a foot.

"So much for baseball camp, Morris! You still can't hit!" Butch yelled.

Chad tossed me my mitt and I jogged out to right. I couldn't even look into the stands. Then, just to make matters worse Butch hit a line drive at me and I misjudged it. The ball flew over my head and Wadski was standing on third before I got the ball back into the infield.

But he didn't score.

As a matter of fact, no one was scoring. Our pitcher, Matt Powell, was doing pretty good himself. Butch's triple was the only hit he'd allowed and as we went into the fourth the score was tied at zip apiece.

That's when Butch really started to pour it on.

He struck out the side with nine pitches and I was one of his victims again. But old Matt came right back and mowed down the Hawks.

Nobody was hitting.

There was still no score in the seventh. I was due to hit third and was determined not to make the last out. Roger leaned over into the dugout.

"Okay, Mikey, this is it."

I tried to smile but my mouth was too dry.

"Coach..."

"No excuses! Just hit the ball."

Talk about pressure. I turned and looked at Kelly. She gave me the clinched fist like she had all the confidence in the world in me. I shook my head in amazement. Hadn't anyone noticed my last two at bats?

Frank Smith went down swinging. Chad had a deep frown on his face as he stepped into the box. Butch didn't waste much time. On his first pitch he smoked Chad on the inside and hit him right between the shoulder blades. My buddy howled in pain and fell behind the plate. He was rolling around and turning blue when I got to him.

"Are you okay?" I asked.

"Oh, man, did that ever hurt," Chad gasped as he rolled over on his back. The pitch had knocked the wind out of him and brought tears to his eyes. Our manager came over to take a look.

"You hurt, Steele?"

"No, sir. Just a little shook up."

Chad got to his feet and slowly walked to first. Wadski had his back to us as he talked to his catcher. Chad could have been dead for all he cared. I looked at Roger and for some reason he was smiling. I couldn't help but smile back. I was still grinning as I got into the batter's box.

"Something funny, Morris?" Butch hissed.

I just kept grinning. All at once I was calm. So what if Butch hit me with a pitch. I'd live through it. I felt myself slip into the zone. The cheering of the crowd seemed to fade away as I cocked my bat. Butch went into his windup. His first delivery was a blazing fastball but I saw it real good. It looked slow enough to reach out and grab. Still, I swung too early and ripped a foul ball down the third base line.

"Way to see it, Mikey," Roger shouted.

Butch seemed stunned by my solid contact. He walked halfway to the plate and sneered at me.

"That was just luck, Morris."

I winked at Butch.

"Yeah, you think so, fella? Lay another one in there like that and we'll see how lucky I was."

Butch couldn't believe his ears.

"Get back up there, nerd."

I stepped to the plate and visualized what was going to happen next. I was going to crush it. Butch went into his windup and gave me a fastball in the same place. It still looked slow and as big as a softball. I timed it perfectly and made contact like I've never made in my life before. The ball went flying out to left field. Everybody just stood and watched as it disappeared over the fence.

My first home run!

"Way to go, Mikey!"

I took my time trotting around the bases. Butch was staring

at me in amazement. I'd hit his best pitch out of the yard and was a hero. A crowd was waiting at home plate to welcome me. All the guys on my team lifted me up on their shoulders and carried me off the field. As I touched back down to earth Kelly gave me a big kiss in front of everybody.

"My hero," she grinned.

Chapter Thirty

It's funny the way things turn out. I dominated Butch for the rest of the summer. All in all I got five homers off him and a bunch of other hits. The dude was mine, and by the end of the season Butch Wadski was a different guy. He didn't swagger as much or try and push me around.

I had his respect.

Besides, I was getting bigger by the second.

Roger had me on a weight lifting program that was really filling me out. Kelly and I dated all the time and she was always asking me to flex. I know it sounds lame but I liked her for that. To my way of thinking it showed she had a real interest in my development.

Then in October, right before the World Series, my mom made the big announcement.

"Roger and I are going to be married."

I'd sort of been expecting it.

"When?"

"The week before Thanksgiving."

"Cool."

It turned out to be a simple ceremony held on the baseball diamond in Kenwood. Roger said something about how it was appropriate since baseball had brought them together. The whole thing was pretty cool, actually. They got married right at home plate. Mom looked beautiful as she came in from second base. I'll never forget the look on her face as she rose over the mound in her wedding dress. It was like she was floating over the infield or something.

The perfect end to an awesome season.

Someday when I'm an old man I'll probably look back on it as the best summer of my whole life. That is, of course, if I don't make it to the Majors and win The Triple Crown. One thing I've learned for sure. You never know what's going to happen.